Thank You

To thank everyone involved in the writing of this book would be impossible. None of us is born into this world knowing much, and what we are and believe is the product of what we were taught or deduce or experience.

By far the greatest influence in my life came from my loving, godly parents (now with the Lord) who prayed for me before I was born, and surrounded me and my siblings with an atmosphere of life lived jointly with us, under and before God. As a result I cannot remember a time when God was not real to me and when my thought life was not open to and in communication with him. For me God has always been my Immanuel who loves me.

Yet interactions with a myriad other people, places, churches, writings and experiences have shaped who I am today, and who I believe God to be, and what I understand is the Gospel revealed in Christ and in the Bible through the Holy Spirit.

Perhaps foremost I should mention my great lifelong friend, Alma Hutton. In school in Stornoway on the Isle of Lewis, we were known as the "Siamese Twins". As iron sharpens iron we have bounced our theology off each other for years and enjoy a union of minds that is truly a gift from God.

I also thank God for other close friends and relatives, as well as Christian churches and organisations. In particular I think of *Christians for Biblical Equality* and the late Catherine Kroeger.

My introduction to Trinitarian Theology came through Baxter Kruger and others at *Perichoresis Ministries* in Jackson, Mississippi. It was not an easy transition for me and I must have read and reread the Bible several times, and the New Testament oftener than that, before I became convinced that the lens through which I had been reading Scripture was somewhat inadequate.

My present home church in Glasgow, Grace Communion International, is a warm loving communion of believers and I am privileged to worship with them.

At a TF Torrance conference in Scotland, Rev Jock Stein found out I was writing a book and kindly offered to read it. His input was invaluable, resulting I believe in a much improved final book. I also wish to thank all who have read the book and given me feedback.

Last but not least, I wish to thank my sister Mary Macdonald, my severest art critic (she likes the cover painting), and a tower of strength to me during the hardest time of my life and even to this day.

Better Than Dreams

(A story exploring God's plans and purposes for us)

by

Christina Campbell

Grosvenor House
Publishing Limited

This book is published by
Grosvenor House Publishing Ltd
28-30 High Street, Guildford, Surrey, GU1 3EL.
www.grosvenorhousepublishing.co.uk

This story is fictional, as are all the extra-biblical
incidents and characters in it.
Scripture taken from THE MESSAGE,
Copyright 1993, 1994, 1995, 1996, 2000, 2001, 2002. Used
by permission of NavPress Publishing Group.

A CIP record for this book
is available from the British Library

ISBN 978-1-78148-900-0

For Grace, my beloved daughter, Edward her husband, and their four children Charis, Campbell, Calista, Colin Angus, who are all a delight to me.

Contents

Introduction

This is a book written for those who are curious about God's rescue plan for humanity, life after death, and what Christ meant when he taught us to pray with him, that God's kingdom would come and that his will would be done on earth as it is in heaven. It is written from the perspective of what is commonly known as Trinitarian Theology. This term is somewhat misleading as most Christians throughout the world, of whatever affiliation or denomination, believe that there is one God in three persons, namely the Father, the Son, and the Holy Spirit, and that the Son became incarnate in Jesus Christ. The difference is that for some of us, this truth takes a precedence in our lives that colours everything else we believe about God, ourselves, and others.

Our starting point is the uncreated God in three persons relating to one another in love, before anything or anybody was ever created. He was never a single person but always three persons. If he had ever been only one person he could only love himself, but narcissism has no place in God's being. The core of God's being is love demonstrated in other-centred relationship. Everything good, that we know and experience, started within this relationship, and flows out of this relationship. We owe our very existence to the overflow of love between the persons of the Trinity who wanted to share their relationship with creatures made in their image, able to love and be loved. The realisation that this divine circle is where all love, camaraderie, fun, kindness, beauty, creativity, excitement, joy, laughter, worship, justice, and everything wholesome originates, together with the biblical revelation of God having planned a good creation that could share in this divine fellowship, makes us look around with new eyes. The whole of every Christian believer's life is lived in, through and because of this circle of love. It is the beginning of all things, the middle of all things, and the end of all things. God planned and created the cosmos and everything in it, and loved it declaring it good. The way the persons of the Trinity relate to each other is the way they relate to us. They know no other way of relating and we do not get to change that, not even through our Fall into sin.

God foresaw the Fall of humanity and refused to be thwarted by evil, determining instead to redeem creation no matter what the cost. This he did in the substitutionary life, death, resurrection, ascension, and continuing intercession of Christ, and in the ongoing work of the Holy Spirit. At every birth, in every baptism, communion celebration, worship service, wedding, funeral, birthday, family meal, new house move, coronation, inauguration, prayer time and all fun times, as well as in every sadness, slander, oppression, torture, murder, rape, problem time, and in all our other human experiences, the Triune God is ever with us. He is Immanuel, God with us, who reveals himself to us in Jesus Christ, sharing himself with us through the Holy Spirit.

Christ when he came to earth struggled to show us what the divine interpersonal relationship of love is really like, and how at one the divine persons really are. Indeed it was not only Christ who took on this task, for at times during his life, the passionate love of the Triune God could not be contained, and broke through for all to see and hear. At his baptism the Holy Spirit came down in the form of a dove on Christ, and the Father shouted his love and admiration for Christ from heaven, "This is my Son, chosen and marked by my love, delight of my life."

Many people have never been introduced to our wonderful God. Many others, when told about him, question the possibility of God being this good. After all, the world as we know it and see it around us, is often a cruel and miserable place.

It was out of my own struggles to understand this tension, and the dynamic of the persons of the Divine Trinity as it impacts on every part of my life, and everyone else's life, that I began to study Scripture anew to see how this is resolved. Up to that point I had understood the main attribute of God to be holiness, outworked towards sinful humanity in wrath and justice that could only be satisfied by the punishment of the guilty party. Christ, I believed, became the substitute that bore the wrath of God and the punishment of death for sinners, at least for those elected to salvation, who trust in Christ. All others I thought were living separated from God, and under his just anger.

Gradually I began to understand that love is the essence of God's being. God never stopped loving us and his creation. The Bible tells us that God is love, but never that God is holiness or justice, which though attributes of God are not the essence of God. Since the Fall we humans are the ones who have become alienated in our minds from God, but he did not become alienated from us, for God was in Christ reconciling the world to himself, not counting our sins against us. God does not change. At the same time we stayed united to Christ, since we were created in him and because he sustains our very lives. Because of this bond Christ was able to take us in union with him down into death and through death to resurrection, as pictured in baptism.

This unchanging love of God towards the world, even after we rebelled against him is a different way of understanding not only the way of salvation, but God and his whole purpose for creating us in the first place. God never changes; he continues to love his wayward children and his desire is that everyone will come to the knowledge of the truth that they are redeemed in Christ. God knows that nothing short of that light dawning in alienated minds will change sinners to become fit to live in his kingdom. That is the good news – the Gospel.

Once I began to accept the absolute centrality of the divine relationship and its impact on all of life, and started sharing this with others, I kept getting asked the same questions over and over. Needless to say they were the same questions I had asked myself, before accepting my present position. Added to that, some people who had come to understand the importance of this way of looking at life, were finding it difficult to explain it to others, and to their children. It was for them that I began writing notes.

As time went on I began to realise that much of what I was trying to explain could better be expressed through a story, and characters who had the same doubts and questions, as those I was being constantly asked.

Some very impressive scholars have written some very heavy tomes answering the theological problems posed by Trinitarian Theology, but valuable as these writings are, they are often technically beyond the grasp of ordinary Christians. Another learned, or not so learned, theological treatise was not what I felt was needed. Even a simplified theological treatise can be tedious for some readers. Perhaps this is why Christ himself used stories to teach the people of his time. Stories tend to give a more comprehensive picture that is not as concentrated as theological propositions. They give us time to reflect on different points of view, without raising our hackles. They seem to give us space to examine our prejudices (we all have these) before we reply in a knee-jerk fashion. They also tend to be more fun, are easier to recall, and we can more easily relate the ideas and insights to our own thinking and lives.

In addition I hope this book will help those who have jeered at me. Whether or not they will ever accept my position, I hope they will at least better understand this teaching, and give up the accusation that because one believes that everyone is included in the atoning work of Christ one believes in universalism, or the belief that everyone will come to trust in Christ for salvation and no one will perish.

"Well, are you saying that everyone is saved but they just don't know it?" I've been asked.

"Conversion can be as simple as that, when the light of what Christ has done hits someone," I answer. "But the work of the Holy Spirit bringing Gospel truth to bear on heart and mind is deep, more than just 'knowing something'. If people do not know the Gospel in this profound sense they are dead to reality, and will continue to live in blindness and darkness as if it were not true."

I sometimes use a story Thomas Erskine narrates, to illustrate the point that our behaviour is directly related to what we believe in the depths of our souls, whether or not it is true. Erskine's story is of a mother whose beloved son went to sea. Not long after he left home the tragic news arrived that her son's ship had been lost, and that there were no survivors. The distraught mother took to her bed, neglected her household, and for two years was barely able to function because of her terrible depression. At the end of two years a letter arrived from her son, to say that he had been cast up on a small uninhabited island, from which he had only recently had been rescued, and that he would be home very soon. Overjoyed the mother forgot her sadness, jumped up, and busied herself preparing for her son's homecoming. What changed her behaviour? Not the fact that her son was alive; he was alive even when she believed he was dead. However, her new conviction (faith) that he was alive changed her behaviour. Only believing the truth of the Gospel can bring us to life, and to being changed to become fit to live in the coming kingdom of our Lord and Saviour, Jesus Christ.

"But don't we have to play a part? Don't we have to repent and ask Christ into our lives? Don't we have to accept Christ?" I am constantly asked.

These and other questions are discussed by the characters in this book. The outline of the story is that of a man who is ill, and who has dreams of life in the coming kingdom, where he is able to interact with the citizens of that new earth and with its king, Immanuel. In his waking hours he talks to his family and friends of his struggles to come to grips with this, for him, new reality of a God and a faith that he had long ago rejected.

Chapter One

Coming to in the Dark

Melvyn came to in the dark. His throat was parched and his chest seared with pain. Gradually he became aware of the clamour. He listened with growing apprehension to the voices: voices of fear, anger, malice, and howls of agony. Vile smells assaulted his nostrils. Sudden flashes of lightening revealed the mayhem. Heaps of writhing bodies were fighting, pushing, tearing, and biting each other in front of a huge smoky dump. From time to time a body was thrown or fell into the acrid glow, or one was pulled from the fire only to be torn apart and devoured limb by limb, by the seething mob.

Melvyn had to escape before he got pulled into this hellish madness. Beyond the inferno, in the lightning flashes, he could just make out some dark mountains ringing the pit on two sides. He must escape to the mountains. He crept further in to the dark shadows. Huge boulders lay scattered around. Furtively he used these rocks to hide himself as he progressed through the darkness, skirting from one hiding place to the next, on his road to safety. His progress was slow. His thirst and

1

pain were unrelenting, but the deafening clamour was too near for comfort. He had to press on into the darkness. He longed to rest but he was afraid to stop. Eventually, through the flashes of light, he thought he could detect the entrance to a cave. Perhaps he could rest there for a time. Pushing on wearily, he at last reached his goal and threw himself on the rocks slabs of the cave. He lay motionless waiting, listening, fearful, but he seemed to be alone and the tumult had somewhat abated.

Where was he? What had happened? Had the country been invaded? Had he been blown into a war zone while in a coma in hospital? This was a far cry from the cool white sheets and the gleaming walls of the hospital ward, where he remembered he had lost consciousness. He remembered Angelina, his wife, holding his hand and crying his name softly over and over: "Melvyn, Melvyn, don't die! Don't leave me alone!"

Where was Angelina now? Selfish woman, why had she not kept beside him? He needed her to take care of him. She should have made sure she stayed beside him.

He closed his eyes and tried to concentrate. What were his options? Perhaps when daylight came he could figure out a way to escape, but then perhaps in daylight they would find him, throw him on the fire and devour him limb by limb. He had no wish to become a human barbecue. No, he would just rest a little and then press on. He slithered exhausted under a protruding ledge and passed out.

Someone rummaging through his pockets woke him with a start, and he fought off his attacker as best he could, with oaths and fists.

"I'm thirsty. I only wanted something to drink or a mint to suck," a voice rasped out of the darkness.

"Angelina?"

"Melvyn, is that you?"

"Yes, of course! Where were you? How did I get here? What do you think you're doing going through my pockets? How could I have a drink or a mint?"

"I know. I don't know. I was dozing in the lounger by your bed, and next thing I knew I woke up in this hellhole."

"I have no idea what happened to me. I think I was in bed and then this. Have you seen them fighting and wasting each other out there?"

"Yes, that's why I came to the rocks to hide!"

"Angelina, as soon as it is morning we've got to get out of here. Here's not safe!"

"I don't think there is a morning here – there's no moon, no stars, and no sun. I think there's been a nuclear war and the world has been destroyed."

"Either that or we've died and gone to hell."

"You know I don't believe in that rubbish, and nor do you!"

"No, but it sure feels like hell!"

"I know, Melvyn, but we haven't lost our minds. We can't be dead or that would be the end of us. We must have survived a nuclear explosion or something. We're not dead but ..."

"I need to get a doctor or I am going to die."

"There are no doctors here. I think we're all going to die."

"I need a drink and the pain is agony. My head is throbbing, and my wound seems to be opening up or pulling apart."

"I need a drink too. That's why I was going through your pockets – anything to drink or suck would do."

"I have nothing to drink! How could I have a drink in my pyjama pockets?"

"I couldn't see you properly in the light of these flashes, and I thought whoever had crawled into my cave had passed out. I couldn't hear any breathing," Angelina protested. "I was desperate enough to drink someone's blood."

Melvyn laughed, "Angelina, that's disgusting! What are we going to do? You've got to help me – I'm in a bad way."

"How can I help you? I can't help myself!"

"You're so useless in an emergency. You might as well clear off. You're no use to me!"

"You clear off! This is my cave. I was here first!"

"I can't think and you're useless."

"Do shut up! You're useless yourself, and a selfish old goat into the bargain. Come to think of it…."

Before she could finish the sentence, an eerie rumble filled the cave and the walls began to shake. Dust fell from the ceiling and the ground moved. A gaping crack began to open up by the entrance of the cave.

Screaming they both jumped and made it outside before large boulders began tumbling from the roof. They had to keep running as the hole widened, and seemed to be following them.

"Quit screaming or they'll hear us!" Melvyn rasped as the ground beneath them seemed to settle again.

Angelina quietened down and began to cry, "What can we do? There's no escape!"

Peering into the darkness Melvyn suggested, "Let's keep to the edge of the rocks and maybe we can find another cave until morning."

"If we get inside another cave we might get buried in another rock-fall," Angelina whined.

"Have you got a better suggestion?" Melvyn asked.

"I suppose not," Angelina conceded, following along.

The ground was rough and they stumbled over rocks and around boulders, with only the occasional lightning flash to help them. They made their way tripping and falling through the darkness, but away from the pit. A huge mountain rose before them and they waited for a lightning flash to help them discern the shortest way around it. Both directions seemed equally long and they hesitated in utter confusion, anxiety, and doubt.

"It doesn't seem to make much difference which way we go," Angelina moaned. "Let's just go to the left."

Melvyn followed her exhausted. They seemed to have been scrabbling along for hours when sneering chuckles stopped them dead. Angelina reached out for Melvyn but he shook her off. Furtively he kept going with Angelina behind. He could hear her laboured breathing. They had almost rounded the base of the mountain when to his horror the smoke of the pit assailed his nostrils, and the screams of the mob reached his ears.

"Oh, no!" he heard Angelina gasp as she caught up with him.

"Nothing for it but to go back and on round the next mountain," Melvyn heard himself say in utter dismay. It had been hard enough getting this far.

The way back was a nightmare, but eventually they rounded the corner on the other side of the next mountain. Again they heard the cackling, sneering laughter, and again they stopped dead in their tracks. The mocking noise seemed to be getting closer but they could see no one. They hurried on terrified. Horror of horrors the smoke of the pit, and the screams of the rabble, again assailed them. They sank to their knees.

"No rest for the wicked! Ha, ha, hah!" screeched a malevolent voice from the darkness. They crouched in terror covering their heads but they heard no more.

"We're going to have to cross the valley at this side, and climb the next range of mountains across from here. It's the only choice left," Melvyn whispered. "Let's hope there's a gap through the fire."

"I don't think I can take another step," Angelina whimpered.

"Please yourself," Melvyn muttered and began clambering forward without a backward glance.

"Wait for me," Angelina pleaded in desperation. Melvyn could hear her frantic gasps and heaving breath but he had no inclination, or energy, to turn round. How he kept going was a puzzle to him. From one footstep to the next, one foot after the other, heaving but not thinking, he had to press on. Once he stopped and sat on a boulder to rest, but the malevolent laughter again cackled around his ears. Angelina was losing ground behind him but he had to press on. She was not ill. Why was she so slow? He felt irritation at her, adding to his utter misery.

Soon they were climbing up the next mountain ridge. The way became harder, and the incline ever steeper. Melvyn was forced to rest every few yards. On one of his longer rests Angelina caught up, but they were both far too exhausted to reproach each other. They shared a boulder and then pressed on. At last they reached the summit and then looked down in horror.

In front of them the smoke of the pit rose in dark plumes from the green glow and orange flames. It seemed to be coming up the mountain to get them until they realised the mountainside itself was sliding down, and spewing out fiery molten rocks. The ground before them was flowing down into the pit. At the same time the raucous laughter they had heard earlier became a deafening roar, and looking behind them they sensed a great company of malevolent beings. Hemmed in on all sides they stood on the precipice until it too began to slide. Melvyn turned to see Angelina. Her mouth gapped wide open as if she was screaming, but he could hear nothing. He was falling, falling into the pit. He could feel the heat and his arms were flailing around helplessly, but he just kept falling, falling forever.

"Hold still! You're all right. It's okay," a nurse was telling him as some orderlies tried to pin him down. He felt the prick of a needle and then lost consciousness.

Chapter Two

Coming to in the Light

Melvyn came to in the light. He felt an arm around his shoulders and wellbeing flooded his body. Clean fresh air filled his lungs, energy and vitality seeped through him, and laughter filled his mouth. Laughter answered his laughter, as in puzzlement he looked around and chortled: "I've no more pain. I'm whole. I'm ..."

The laughter around him became singing:

"Look! Look! God has moved into the neighbourhood, making his home with men and women! They're his people, he's their God. He'll wipe every tear from their eyes. Death is gone for good – tears gone, crying gone, pain gone – all the first order of things gone."

He looked from the direction of the singing to the hand still holding his shoulder, and heard the words: "Look! I am making everything new."

Not daring to lift his eyes higher he questioned: "Who are you?"

"I am A to Z. I'm the Beginning. I'm the Conclusion. From Water-of-Life Well I give freely to the thirsty."

"But I don't believe in God!" Melvyn protested.

The voice continued: "the feckless and faithless, degenerates and murderers, sex peddlers and sorcerers, idolaters and all liars – for them it's Lake Fire and Brimstone. Second death."

The arm left his shoulder and the presence was gone. Melvyn shuddered. He began remembering something.

A pleasant voice beside him announced:

"I'm not going to breathe life into men and women endlessly. Eventually they're going to die; from now on they can expect a lifespan of 120 years. Why do you insist on going against the grain?"

Melvyn turned to look at the voice that spoke to him. The nearby bushes rustled gently in the breeze, but he saw no one. All the laughing singers had gone too.

He sat down and studied the scene before him. He was on a hillside, the day was young, the air incredibly fresh, and by his side a pristine water-spring gurgled and splashed over some large flat rocks. Before him stretched a park land of some sort, with a fair sized lake in the middle, skirted by what looked like a running track. Presently he saw some joggers bumping along the track, disappearing into the shade of some clumped trees, then reappearing again where the trees thinned out. To the far side of the lake stretched grassy meadows, and a large palatial looking house. In the distance rose range after range of impressive mountains, the tallest capped with snow, though here on the hillside the warm breeze and brightly coloured wild flowers attested to the season being early summer.

Perhaps he should go exploring. He dipped his foot into the stream and the fast-flowing coolness sprayed his legs. He got up, stepped onto a submerged rock, cupped his hands and tasted the cool clear water.

"One could make a fortune bottling this stuff," he thought.

Feeling good, feeling strong, and more alive than he had ever felt in his life, he sprinted down the hillside and across the grassy meadow, just in time to join a couple of joggers.

"Hi! Want to join us?" asked the man.

"Sure, if you don't mind," Melvyn responded.

"Wow, what kind of surface is this?" Melvyn asked. "It feels like cork."

"It is a type of cork. A band of engineers designed it recently and it feels really good. Jogging, running, walking, anything, it's really gentle on the joints."

"I should say! It's marvellous! I've never run on anything like this before," Melvyn mused admiringly. "Is it okay for anyone to use it? I would have thought you'd have to belong to a club or something to run here."

His companions looked at him quizzically and chuckled, "Yeah, anyone can use it, and it's absolutely free."

"I expect your taxes are pretty high then?"

Waves of laughter greeted his question and a retort of: "Very funny!"

They circled the track several times and then his companions turned into the much narrower path leading up to the large house.

"Coming for a bite to eat?" they invited.

"This is your place?" Melvyn queried.

Again the couple looked at him and then at each other, bemused. "Yes, it's ours," the man retorted.

"And yours too," the woman added.

"It's very kind of you. Thank you!" Melvyn stammered.

They slowed to a walk. "I'm Jessie and this is Ewan," said the woman as she held out her hand.

"I'm Melvyn, pleased to meet you!"

By this time they were entering a large pillared court room filled with long stone tables and benches. Huge potted plants and trellises of fragrant flowers scented the air. In the centre a fountain gushed water from pitchers held by pairs of abstract bronze sculpted animals. A couple of very beautiful winged harpists played soft music in the background. Several diners were seated eating and chatting quietly together. Several waved to Jessie and Ewan as they led the way into the house.

An archway led straight into the kitchens. Going inside an amazing plethora of aromas wafted over them. In front of them, spread on massive counters, there seemed to be every kind of food known to man. At cookers, ovens, fires, barbecues, hundreds of cooks poured over pots and dishes. The newcomers were greeted with beaming smiles and pleas to just try this new dish, that new bread, this new salad, that extraordinary soup, or any of the heavenly desserts.

Jessie and Ewan urged Melvyn to sample whatever took his fancy. A waiter appeared by their side, noted their preferences, and after seating them in the courtyard went inside to fill their orders. Warm wet towels were brought out to refresh the guests, and then a small army of waiters carried out trays of steaming dishes: vegetables, meats, fish, and fowl. They arranged their individual plates so artistically that it almost seemed a shame to tuck into them.

Something kept Melvyn from asking who paid for it all. It would seem crass. There was something holy, almost sacramental in the way this food was prepared and served. Delight seemed to ooze from the chefs, the waiters, the servers and the served. Melvyn ate in awe, every morsel an exquisite experience of colour, flavour, texture, all blending wonderfully on his tongue, and in his mouth as he slowly savoured and swallowed this amazing food. Where did these chefs come from? Where did they get their ingredients? How did they come by such servers and waiting staff? Setting down his coffee cup he could scarcely talk. Looking at his companions he whispered, "That was beyond compare."

"Yes, such passion for perfection. They just keep getting better and better!"

"Where do they get the produce?"

"Come and see!"

Ewan led the way through an alcove by the side of the kitchens, down a wide cloistered walkway to huge walled gardens that seemed to stretch endlessly behind the house. Adjoining the house itself were conservatories containing vast arrays of exotic flowers, fruits, and vegetables. These were tended by gardeners who were digging, planting, watering, harvesting. They were all more than happy to share their knowledge and expertise with the visitors.

The same was true of the walled gardens. Bevies of passionate gardeners tended plot after plot of top quality flowers, fruits, and vegetables. They too were pleased to answer the visitors' questions, point out aspects of special interest, while in turn accepting the compliments and admiration of the visiting trio.

Eventually a path led them out of the gardens through a patch of woodland into a picnic area, and car park. The cars all seemed top of the range; many were vintage and all looked as if they had just been driven out of a show room.

"Pick a car!" Jessie invited Melvyn with a laugh.

Melvyn laughed too. "Sure thing! I'll just have that silver vintage beauty over there."

To his astonishment Jessie and Ewan headed for the car, opened the doors and asked if he would like to drive. The key was already in the ignition.

"So this is your car?" Melvyn asked as the other two got in. They laughed.

"If you take the road to the right when you get out of the car park, it will take us into the countryside where you can examine the sheep and cattle. It's a very pleasant drive and then we can go to the dairies, the grain fields, and the vineyards afterwards, if you like," Jessie offered.

Melvyn turned the key and the car purred to life. Slowly he drove towards the exit, and then to the right as Jessie had suggested. He could hardly believe he was behind the wheel of such a magnificent car. They breezed through the meadow lands of emerald green grass, dotted with wild flowers and bordered by hedgerows of tangled hawthorn, brambles, and wild roses. Sleek, contented cattle and sheep grazed in the fields, or sat chewing the cud. Deer, ostrich, and many other game animals and fowl could be spotted among clumps of ancient trees, or lying beside quiet streams and pools. None of the animals seemed wary of the car, or of the other animals, or indeed of anything in their environment.

Gradually the road veered left skirting a huge lake where boats of every vintage were sailing about; some were fishing boats.

"Our supplies of fresh fish," Ewan explained. "There, the dairies are just up ahead. Pull off to the right up the next driveway!"

Simple buildings of gleaming white marble stretched as far as the eye could see. Alongside the backs of the buildings were open sided milking sheds leading straight to fields of milking animals; some Melvyn recognized and some he did not. They parked the car and wandered through the dairies. Milk, cream, butter, yogurt and cheeses of all descriptions were being processed in the buildings, some still at the experimental stage, while others were being matured in various ways. Samples were slivered from a multiplicity of the cheeses for their comments. Each seemed more flavourful than the last. Again those at work were at pains to share their insights and passion for their produce, with the three visitors. Eventually they decided to return to the car, and continue their sightseeing around the lake.

Part way around the placid water, they stopped at a cafe with a veranda overlooking the lake. Melvyn had a soft drink while his companions sipped fruit tea. As a light rain began to dance on the lake top some of the boats made for shore. Soon a raucous crowd from the boats joined them in the cafe.

As soon as the rain stopped the trio continued along the road skirting the lake. On the far side, leaving the dairies behind, the meadows rose sharply and turned to parkland, then to forest, and gradually to grasslands. Exotic animals and birds viewed them and other visitors, but showed no signs of being perturbed. People wandered among the lions, tigers, elephants, hippos, and other wild animals, stroking, petting, and wrestling playfully with them, apparently without a care in the world. Melvyn stopped the car while a magnificent male lion, flanked by a couple of young zebras, crossed the road. Melvyn declined the offer of a stroll among the animals.

A mountain rose before them but a wide pass took them to mile after mile of rolling wheat and grain fields. The methods used to work the fields varied from ploughs and oxen, to the most modern machinery. Melvyn was absolutely fascinated, especially since the crops all looked equally healthy. Further along the road they came upon flooded fields where rice crops were being planted, again using a variety of farming methods that ranged from the primitive labour intensive methods of times long past, to the computer managed methods of modern times.

As with the farm implements, the vehicles they passed on the road included not only modern cars and busses, but carriages, buggies, horses, camels, elephants and even a dog drawn trap. Bicycles, tricycles, and tandems of various vintages were all in use. From time to time they passed interesting looking towns and villages. At one of these they stopped to watch some artists at work in their studios and workshops. Melvyn admired the work of one very fine silversmith who was putting the finishing touches to an intricate buckle, not only with skill but also with obvious pride. Catching Melvyn's eye she asked, "Do you like this buckle?"

"It is the most beautiful piece of silver work I have ever seen," Melvyn replied.

"Then I would love you to have it. Please take it!"

"I couldn't possibly …" Melvyn protested. The woman looked at him shocked.

"If you like it, take it. It is with pleasure I give it to you," she said holding out the beautiful silver buckle.

"I don't know what to say. Thank-you very much," Melvyn stammered. She smiled.

"Can I offer you any of my work?" she asked turning to Jessie and Ewan. Jessie chose a delicate filigree bracelet set with garnets and smoky quartz. Ewan chose a heavy silver ring set with a large lapis lazuli. Julia, the silversmith, looked delighted as she waved good bye to them and returned to her work.

Somewhere in the middle of the village a man joined them. Ewan and Jessie stopped and looked at him expectantly.

"I'll take Melvyn from here. I expect you'll want to get back to your golf tournament, Jessie, and no doubt your friends at the library will be glad to pick your brains, Ewan. How is the research going anyway?" he asked.

"It's going very well indeed, thanks!" Ewan beamed.

Jessie and Ewan got back into the car and with a, "Be seeing you!" They had left Melvyn in the care of the stranger.

Taking charge, the stranger put his hand on Melvyn's shoulder and pointed him to a narrow path that led into some wasteland. Melvyn remembered that touch, and with it a certain mixture of excitement and trepidation.

"Melvyn, I have much to show you if you have eyes to see and ears to hear," a deep calm voice spoke into his heart.

"I know I am dreaming. This is not real. You are not real. I must be very sick but I don't want to wake up!"

Melvyn protested cheerfully. "This is the best dream I've ever had."

"Wake up is exactly what you need to do. For too long, you have been living in a dream world of unreality, blind and dead to all right thinking," the stranger replied.

"Are you trying to tell me this dream is real and you really exist?"

"I am."

"Prove it then!" a defiant Melvyn challenged.

"I-AM-WHO-I-AM, Melvyn."

"How do you know me?" Melvyn queried.

"Know you? I made you. I fashioned you in your mother's womb and breathed my life into you. Every breath you take is my breath. I am the one who called you and all creation out of dark nothingness into the light of being. If I were to withdraw my support from you, or from any part of creation, you and it would slide back into nothingness. Outside of me there is only darkness, decay, death, chaos, and emptiness. The purpose of creation is life lived to the full. Our plans for you are for good and not evil. "

A choir above them began to sing:

"I know what I'm doing. I have it all planned out – plans to take care of you, not abandon you, plans to give you the future you hope for. When you call on me, when you come and pray to me, I'll listen. When you come looking for me you'll find me. Yes, when you get serious about finding me and want it more than anything else, I'll make sure you won't be disappointed."

Melvyn trembled. For a moment he remembered another time, another place, another dream.

Chapter Three

Coming to in the Hospital

Melvyn felt himself being pulled in two different directions at the same time, through a deep and terrifying darkness.

"Help me! Help me!" he shouted as he gasped for breath and flung his arms about wildly. He woke up screaming and flailing about.

Angelina started crying, "It wasn't meant to be like this. I can't stand this. I've got to get out of here. My friends Emma and Mabel live only ten miles away. I'll phone them. I must have some time for myself away from all this."

Melvyn begged weakly, "Don't leave me! Please stay and help me! I need you!"

Angelina sniffed but became adamant, "I've got to look after myself. I'm not strong. I'm going to my friends. I can't do this! I'm not well enough to do this! I hate hospitals! You know I'm not strong! The staff will look after you. Please don't ask me to stay! I just can't!"

Angelina disappeared into the bathroom. Melvyn could hear her sobbing, and then phoning her friends.

Next he could hear her fixing her makeup, and packing up her accoutrements. She came out and announced, "I'm off to Emma and Mabel's for the day." She finished her packing, and without further ado picked up her bag, and made for the door.

"You're really going to leave me alone, Angelina?" Melvyn's voice shook.

Angelina bit her lip, "Sorry! I have to. I'll see you tomorrow." With that she was gone.

Tears rolled unheeded from Melvyn's eyes and over the sides of his cheeks.

"God help me," Melvyn whispered, "even if I don't believe in you!"

A tall graceful figure flitted across the room, bent over his bed and kissed his forehead.

"How are you feeling, Dad? Where is Angelina?" she asked.

"Can you stay with me, Karen? I feel awful and so alone. Angelina has gone off to her friends. She says she needs time for herself," Melvyn replied.

"I can stay, Dad. Don't cry! Can I get you anything?" Karen asked.

"Just stay with me. How long can you stay?"

"I can stay a few days. Adam is looking after the children and his parents are helping. He said I should take as long as I needed. He's being very kind and understanding."

"That's good! I'm so tired. It's good of you to come and see me. If you don't mind I think I'll sleep now."

Melvyn slept fitfully for part of the day. The usual bevy of doctors, nurses, and orderlies came and went. Karen tried to find out as much as she could about her father's condition, treatment, and prognosis. She knew he had had a partial gastrectomy for stomach cancer, earlier that month. A couple of the nearby lymph nodes had also been found to be cancerous. He had been sent home a few weeks later, but he soon had to be readmitted with fever and terrible pain. He was hooked up to antibiotics, strong pain killers, and various other medicines for a serious infection. He had been scanned for possible internal leakage at the site where his stomach had been reattached to his intestine, but nothing unusual had shown up. He had obviously contracted an infection, but nobody seemed to know exactly how this could have happened, or why her father had relapsed, and was so ill. He had been on the way to recovery when he left the hospital. Nobody seemed to have the full picture.

Karen lived a hundred miles away, and it was only from Melvyn's brother that Karen had found out that her father had been readmitted to hospital. Angelina had not bothered to let her know. Angelina had never liked Karen, and for some reason seemed threatened by her.

As the day progressed Melvyn's condition seemed to worsen. He became delirious and imagined himself trying to get out of a swimming pool. It took all Karen's strength to keep him on the edge of the bed, and attached to all his tubes. He shook uncontrollably and then began to gag and vomit. Karen called for help but nobody came. Desperately she clung to her father and stretched for the alarm cord, while trying to keep her father from falling to the floor. His ramblings frightened her. A nurse eventually came and helped her get her father cleaned up and back into bed. The nurse then sedated him, and he slept.

Karen called her husband, Adam, and spoke to her children. She then dashed to the hospital cafe and grabbed a sandwich and a drink. By midnight Angelina had not called, and Karen imagined it was now too late for her to call. Karen pulled out the hospital lounger, lay down, and tried to sleep.

She woke early while Melvyn was still sleeping fitfully. She quietly washed and again dashed down to the cafe, and brought back some breakfast and a sandwich for lunch. Her father was still sleeping. She slowly ate a bacon roll, some yogurt and fruit, washed down with orange juice. Feeling better she took out her Bible and began to read to herself from the beginning of John's first letter. Moved by the beautiful ancient words she decided to read aloud:

"From the very first day, we were there, taking it all in – we heard it with our own ears, saw it with our own eyes, verified it with our own hands. The Word of Life appeared right before our eyes; we saw it happen! And now we're telling you in most sober prose that what we witnessed was, incredibly, this: The infinite Life of God himself took shape before us.

We saw it, we heard it, and now we're telling you so that you can experience it along with us, this experience of communion with the Father and his Son, Jesus Christ. Our motive for writing is simply this: We want you to enjoy this, too. Your joy will double our joy!

This, in essence, is the message we heard from Christ and are passing on to you: God is light, pure light; there's not a trace of darkness in him."

Melvyn slept on as she read.

"What do you think you're doing? You know Melvyn doesn't want to listen to those primitive lies. It's all garbage," Angelina yelled from the door.

"He's asleep," Karen sighed warily.

"You know you shouldn't be here. He doesn't want you. You just upset him," Angelina continued accusingly.

"I'll let my father tell me that," Karen replied defensively.

"I'm telling you and that should be good enough for you! I'm his wife. You need to listen to me! You'll do what you're told! You can leave now!" Angelina yelled louder than ever.

"Excuse me, in case you haven't noticed I'm an adult, and you are not my mother. I don't have to obey you," Karen replied firming her tone.

"What's wrong? Why are you yelling?" Melvyn asked hazily, wakened by the raised voices.

"It's okay, Dad. I'm leaving," Karen said shakily.

"Karen, please don't go! I need you here. I want you here," Melvyn pleaded.

"Don't worry, Dad! I'll be back later," she reassured him.

"Wait! I need to talk to you. When are you going home?" Angelina asked.

"On Friday afternoon," Karen replied.

"Well you can't! You're going to have to stay here until Saturday," Angelina fumed irrationally, not seeming to recollect the contradiction between this and her previous outburst. "I'm tired and I've got to have time off. My friends want me to go out with them on Friday."

Angelina narrowed her eyes as she cornered Karen, but she lowered her voice somewhat, "You'll have to stay, you know."

"My children need me. I can't leave them that long," Karen explained.

"Your father needs you and you'll have to stay!" Angelina's voice was again getting heated.

"Can you stay with me Friday night, Angelina?" Melvyn asked. "Karen needs to get back to her kids."

Angelina stalked past Karen, who was still at the doorway. Melvyn pleaded, "Please come back for Friday night, Angelina!" Angelina stalked out promising nothing. She had never been able to hide the fact that she did not like Karen.

Karen could contain herself no longer. She sank into a chair and burst into tears.

"Why is she so horrible to me? What have I ever done to her?"

"Nothing, Angelina's just under a lot of stress," Melvyn excused.

"She has no right! She's just mean and selfish," Karen sobbed.

"I'm sorry, Dad! I don't mean to upset you. I'll be myself in a minute. If Angelina won't stay with you Friday night, I could phone Mom to come over from Canada to look after the children."

Stella, Karen's mother and Melvyn's first wife, had already offered to look after the children, to give Karen time to be with her father, whose chances of survival were not brilliant. Karen had not broached the subject with him until now.

"Absolutely not! I don't even want that woman to know that I'm ill, and I certainly don't want her looking after me!" Melvyn shouted.

"She wouldn't be looking after you or anywhere near you. She would be looking after the children," Karen tried to reason with him.

"No! No, I don't want her having anything to do with me!"

Karen knew it would be useless to argue further with her father, and dropped the subject.

That day went past for Karen in a blur of misery. Her father was slightly better and he slept again from time to time. However when he woke his mind often wandered. He imagined himself in a hot tub and tried to get out of bed. Karen feared he would injure himself and pull out all his tubes.

Help and information from the hospital that day was less forthcoming than the previous day. Apparently, on her way out, Angelina had ordered the staff not to talk about Melvyn, to his mentally unstable daughter. However, that night Janice, a kindly, no nonsense nurse was on duty. She looked in on Melvyn, checked his vital signs, temperature and blood pressure, and let Karen know that her father's fever had subsided. It was not unusual for someone with a high fever to be delirious at times, she told Karen. He was responding to the antibiotics, and other medicines. Savvy and experienced, she also noted Karen's weariness and her motherly heart went out to the younger woman, who looked so wan and troubled.

"You go on down to the cafe and have some dinner, my dear. I'll make sure your Dad is okay," she coaxed kindly.

"Well, if you're sure. Thanks, Nurse Janice!"

Later, as Karen dozed on the ward lounger, she heard the phone ring incessantly at the nurse's station. Time after time Nurse Janice answered the phone between her other duties. From time to time Karen heard exasperated sighs, and snatches of conversation.

"Madam, I can't give you that information. As I told you before …"

"Madam, I don't have time for this. I have patients to look after. Hospital policy is that progress reports be given to only one relative. That relative can then inform whomever about the state of the patient."

"Madam, I don't believe you are the patient's wife. If you were his wife you would be with him now. He is very ill."

"You do that, Madam. I have no time for this. As I said before I have patients to look after. Bye!"

Karen smiled to herself, realizing who was pestering the staff. She soon relaxed and fell asleep.

Next morning Melvyn did seem somewhat better. It was the surgeon's day for visiting. Being a top doctor in his field and proud of it, he strutted about accompanied by junior doctors and some very deferential staff.

"I'm sorry you had to be readmitted, Mr Reed, but you are on the mend now, I believe," the surgeon informed Melvyn. "You must know that at this stage much of your recovery depends on you. You have to make an effort to get well. You need to get up and eat something! I'll see you again in a few days. I think that by Friday you may be well enough to go home, and then in a month's time we'll check up on you and discuss further treatment."

Melvyn looked green and gagged but some of his old fight came back.

"Eat something? Make an effort to get better? You're not the one who has had the operation. Have you ever had an operation to remove half your stomach?"

"My father has been very ill," Karen sounded shocked as she addressed the surgeon. "He's been delirious on and off for a couple of days."

"He's on the mend now," the surgeon replied, kindly enough.

"I'll be back in a few days and I had better see some improvement. If you give up now, Mr Reed, you'll just die!" he warned Melvyn.

"That was a bit of a show!" Karen quipped to her father after he had gone. "What an attentive retinue!"

"Haughty, but he is the best," her father admitted.

Melvyn sighed and soon afterwards fell into a deep sleep. A whirlwind seemed to be whisking him away through a long tunnel. He seemed to be flying but the sensation was not unpleasant. He realized he had two companions, one at each side holding him by the elbows.

Chapter Four

Immanuel's Kingdom

Melvyn was gently dropped on the hillside of his initial pleasant dream. The air, as before, was warm and invigorating. The pristine stream played joyfully over the rocks as if glad to see him, and a sense of delight filled Melvyn's whole being. The grass rustled beside him. He could see no one but he felt sure he was not alone. A passage of Scripture he had learned as a boy came back unbidden to his mind:

"The created world itself can hardly wait for what's coming next. Everything in creation is being more or less held back. God reins it in until both creation and all the creatures are ready and can be released at the same moment into the glorious times ahead. Meanwhile the joyful anticipation deepens."

"What does it all mean? Is there really a God? Is there more to life than I can see? Have I been suppressing reality all my life? Am I dreaming again? I'm not sure of anything anymore ..." Melvyn admitted aloud.

Again he felt a presence beside him. Looking around he saw a man approaching him. The man slid down the grassy bank and sat beside him.

"We meet again!" Melvyn ventured.

"Not really! I am always with you," the man replied.

"What is your name?" Melvyn asked.

"Immanuel," the man replied.

"I am so confused. I don't know what is real anymore. I know I am dreaming and I have been ill. Perhaps this dream is showing me reality, or perhaps it is all just an illusion brought on by delirium. I don't see how I can ever be sure of anything again. What is it all about? What is the truth?" Melvyn stammered incoherently.

"Melvyn, I am the Truth, and the truth is that I have made you with a loving yearning inside of you, that only I can satisfy. You were made for love and to share in my love. I am Love and I give my children my love, so that they can love me and each other. Your life is tied up in mine, as my life is tied up in my Father's, through the Spirit. I love you, and long for you to see things as they really are," Immanuel explained.

"I'm afraid that makes no sense to me. When I grew up I rejected the Bible as mostly fables, and exaggeration. It never made sense to me. I don't even know where to start. My life has often been a mess but I think it has been honest. I live by the light of reason, and believe the universe just happened by chance," Melvyn added somewhat defensively.

Immanuel smiled, "If the only light you have is darkness, how great is that darkness! You believe your reason is the product of a mindless, unguided process but you still trust it?"

Melvyn smiled too, "I suppose if you put it like that maybe I don't; I'm not expressing myself very well."

Melvyn was distracted. He felt strangely alive, loved, and full of peace. He did not want to change anything at the moment. He would think things through later. "If this is the opiate of the people it feels wonderful," he wryly admitted to himself. "It beats any other life hands down."

"Do you really want to know the meaning of your life, and the purpose of your history?" asked Immanuel.

"I have been seeking clarity on that all my life. I've settled for a liberal secularism. We believe we should live at peace with each other, and try to make life better for each other. Then we accept we will die, and that is the end of us," Melvyn explained. "The most we can hope for is that we will leave the world a better place for the next generation, than when we entered it."

"How has that worked for you, Melvyn?"

"To be honest not very well," Melvyn admitted. "Even my marriages have been a failure. I haven't made the world a better place and now I'm ill and dying, and there's no chance left for improvement."

"That's because it was never left up to you, or to any mere mortal, to set the world to rights again. You are starting in the wrong place. You are starting with yourself and humanity, and hoping to get them to pull themselves up by their bootstraps. You have to start with my Father, with the Holy Spirit, and with me, and then everything will fall into place. Only I am able to pull humanity out of the pit they have dug for themselves. I alone am able to transfer them into the divine circle of love, where they belong, sharing my glory and my life."

"How can you do this? Is it not too late for me and countless others?"

"I suppose you're asking if I have given up on you – if I have stopped loving you and others, who do not believe in me? I am God and I do not change. My love sometimes expresses itself in wrath and discipline, but its aim is always corrective and loving. Anyone can choose eternal death and have it – no one's will is violated, but it is not my will that any human being should be lost in the darkness."

"You're supposed to be all powerful; you could have made us do whatever you wanted," Melvyn interrupted.

"Wanted? We did not want puppet love. We are love, and love does not bully. Our purpose (that is my Father's, the Spirit's, and mine) is the adoption of the human race into our family. We wanted to share our love with all of you – something like the desire we put in a human couple's marriage, when they want to share their love by having children. We wanted real love, not a fake forced love. For real love to exist and flourish, a true knowing and understanding has to evolve. As the eternal God we have no beginning, and we had no experience of what it is like to be created beings. To give love a chance to become reciprocal it was decided that I should become human, a divine human mediator. I would share with the Father, through the Spirit, the being and sensitivities of created humanity, and I would let humanity share in my divine family circle. Humans were united to us from the beginning, when we breathed our life into them at their creation.

Though we made humanity good, we had to give them the freedom to choose evil. Of course, we warned them ahead of time, that the consequences of choosing evil would be death."

"But you must have known the risk of leaving them a choice?"

"Oh, yes! We were under no illusions. We knew humanity would choose evil. We prepared for the Fall of humanity in the planning stages of creation. We had no intentions of letting our good plans for humanity fail. We had a rescue plan ready to be put in place right away."

Melvyn remembered the story of the Fall.

"Were you not angry that humanity was duped, and chose to believe an evil tempter rather than you?"

"We were exceedingly angry! Our precious children had been corrupted and were suffering terribly. All our good creation had been spoiled and was reverting to darkness, decay, and chaos. Humanity was in great danger. When evil invades a person's mind, less and less of the person is left. As soon as humanity ate of the tree of the knowledge of good and evil, humanity become diseased in mind and body. There was then the further danger that humanity would eat of the tree of life, and remain in their fallen state forever."

"What did you do?"

"We expelled them from the garden as quickly as possible. The rescue plan was already in place, as I told you. They were created in me and united to me they live, move, and have their being. Like a living branch in a vine, human life is sustained by me. If a branch gets cut off it withers and dies, while the vine continues to live. However, if the vine dies all the branches die with it. Creation, including humanity, is so united to me that whatever happens to me affects them also. When I died, you and all humanity died with me. I am your life and the keeper of your life. When I rose from the dead, you and all humanity rose with me."

Thinking of the horror of a crucifixion death Melvyn asked, "How could you even think of putting yourself at the mercy of humanity, in the certain knowledge of eventual torture and such a horrible death?"

"I could not let my beloved children slip back, and decay into nothingness. The Spirit wrapped me without measure in my Father's love. On several occasions I was strengthened by my Father's voice bursting through directly from heaven, his dwelling place, exclaiming his love and delight in me. I was not alone in my sufferings, and I could see the joy that I would experience eventually – the joy of my children living life to the full on a new earth, in the age to come."

"You didn't come to earth right away. Why did you wait away for so long?"

"When humanity fell, their thinking became distorted and foolish. They were so frightened and guilt-ridden they imagined we would now hate them, and punish them; so they ran away and hid in the bushes. Silly children! We do not change nor do we let evil thwart our good plans. The way forward became messy and painful but never hopeless; we had our plan. It was a plan that involved the maturing of the human race. We had to burn new concepts into their psyches to bring their thinking into alignment with ours, with truth."

"I still don't get why you had to die. Surely there was another way?"

"No, there was only one way and I am that Way. Humanity became fatally diseased in mind and body, and to bring them back to health and life they had to die, and be resurrected. There is no cure for sin but death. The clay had to be smashed down and reworked into a new creation. They couldn't ever resurrect themselves; they could only be resurrected in me. I told you before that humanity only exists and has life because I share my life with them. I had to become human, mortal, so that I could die. When I died all humanity died with me, and when I rose all humanity rose with me. My death broke the power of sin, and I broke the power of death. Everything is being made new."

"But I was taught as a child that we humans have an immortal soul," Melvyn interjected.

Immanuel laughed, "That is a false idea picked up from Greek philosophers along with other pagan ideas. Only God has life in himself, and we are the only ones who breathe life into anything and make it live. Nothing outside of me can live by itself, and when I died all creation died with me."

Above them angel voices rang out:

"Our old way of life was nailed to the Cross with Christ, a decisive end to that sin-miserable life – no longer at sin's beck and call! What we believe is this: If we get included in Christ's sin-conquering death, we also get included in his life-saving resurrection. We know that when Jesus was raised from the dead it was a signal of the end of death-as-the-end. Never again will death have the last word. When Jesus died, he took sin down with him, but alive he brings God down to us. From now on, think of it this way: Sin speaks a dead language that means nothing to you; God speaks your mother tongue, and you hang on every word. You are dead to sin and alive to God. That's what Jesus did."

"I am the beginning of the whole new creation. My body is the first resurrected body – the kind of body that can never die again, and that my people will have in the new world. There is a lot, lot more to the story, Melvyn, but I intend to let my brothers and sisters share it with you, using theatre, cinema, and drama. We have so many researchers, writers, actors, costume makers, illustrators, set designers, lighting specialists, camera people and a host of other artists and engineers to make our shows truly authentic. Many of the characters from the real stories have been interviewed by the actors and actresses taking part. Those involved in the productions have received input on the details of the historical settings, the clothes worn at the time, plus the dynamics and politics of particular incidents, and even in some cases the actual words used," Immanuel continued.

"It all sounds fascinating. Where do we go?" Melvyn asked.

"Come and see!" Immanuel urged.

Chapter Five

Kingdom Life

They got up, crossed the stream and headed in the opposite direction from the running track. In no time they had climbed a small ridge and far below them they could see what looked like a huge, three decked, ancient warship being built in a field. Floating airborne seats that looked like clouds held crowds of spectators. They got in one and Melvyn noticed the controls looked like golden harps. Immanuel laughed at Melvyn's discomfort.

"It's an in-joke! Many people on earth think folks here just sit on clouds playing golden harps. Someone thought it would be funny to create theatre seats that made fun of the caricature."

"That is funny," Melvyn agreed, "but in spite of that, functional too."

"Yes, the view is good and we can hear everything that goes on."

Some actors were jeering at the builders: "Noah, how are you going to get your boat to the water?"

"Noah, nobody is going to get on that boat with you. Why have you made it so big?"

"Noah, you're wasting your time. There's never been a flood here before. The sky is as blue as ever. Noah, you're crazy!"

"Noah, it's been over a century. When are you going to give it up? Nobody believes your silly tales of doom. Stop your silly preaching!"

To these and other jeers Noah patiently answered that God had told him to build the ark, and that those who believed God should join him. He warned them, that the consequence of all the evil and injustice among humanity grieved the Lord exceedingly. God was going to have to destroy everything and start his creation over again. He did not want a world like this and he was being very patient, giving people year after year a chance to change. The time was getting short. The people just laughed and shook their heads.

Immanuel explained, "This is the story of God's love for his creation. You will recall that after humanity was exiled from Eden we clothed them and still cared for them. We kept trying to keep up communication with them, but they became less and less human, less and less able to hear us and respond to us, and more and more depraved. Murder, rape, pillage, slavery, idolatry, greed, and every kind of injustice increased on earth, until we were appalled by the degeneration. It was heart-breaking."

Melvyn asked, "Why did you let evil escalate? Why did you not put your plan into action sooner? Why did you let the people go so far?"

They had just watched the ship being loaded with supplies. Now the amazing sight of congregating animals, birds, and insects, running, walking, creeping, flying into their quarters on the ark, put an end to conversation for the time being. Noah meanwhile was making one last plea to the crowds gathered to watch the spectacle of the animals entering the ark. As before, his message fell on deaf ears. Finally Noah and his family climbed up the gangplank into the ark, and the door was shut.

The skies were blue and cloudless as the crowds began to disperse. Suddenly, the weather changed dramatically. Dark clouds appeared above, and water came from everywhere and everything, with terrifying ferocity. People were lifted and swept along by the raging torrent. Some shouted for Noah to open the door but the tumult of the waters would have made it impossible to hear anybody. In vain people and animals fled to higher ground and then to even higher ground. The strongest and fittest made it far up the mountains but still the waters surged and rose. Soon the ark rose too and floated on the surface of the water, while the towns around were blotted out in the deluge.

When the raging waters eventually calmed down the massive ark could be seen bobbing like a cork, on the watery wasteland. Even the highest mountains were submerged. They watched the story progress, climaxing in the Covenant promises given by God to Noah and humanity, and sealed with a beautiful rainbow spanning the sky.

As they descended from their airborne floating seats, Immanuel got back to answering Melvyn questions. "As I indicated before," Immanuel explained, "we had to give people freedom to be themselves. By letting things deteriorate in this way we wanted to show humanity where their idolatry and independence would lead them. Instead they got so blind in their wickedness,

they could not or would not see, and we knew we had to
start over with the one family on earth that still had ears
to hear us. All humanity left outside the ark died and
their spirits went to Hades. Not that we gave up on
them or stopped loving them, for I myself went and
preached the truth to them after my death. There was no
cure for those people living at the time of Noah, or
indeed at any time, but death and resurrection in
me. The ark was to become picture language to later
generations, as an image of the Gospel. It showed rescue
through my baptism of death, burial, and resurrection,
in union with humanity. Only death and resurrection
to new life in me could save humanity from total
disintegration. Of course, those who insist on staying in
Hades for whatever reason, whether deliberate blindness, pathetic defiance, or idolatry of one kind or
another, are left there as that is their choice. If they
continue to walk further and further away from me they
become prey to the adversary Satan, who is like a
roaring lion always looking to devour a stray human. By
devour I mean that evil spreads in such humans like a
disease, until eventually there is no humanity left in
them, and to all intents and purposes they become one
with Satan."

"As I recollect from the Bible history, things did not
take long, after the flood, to deteriorate again as the
human population increased," Melvyn interjected.

"You're right! In no time they were building the
Tower of Babel, but let me take you to a princess who
will tell you the next stage of our plan for a whole new
world."

Melvyn was whisked away to an ancient looking
oasis. There he was taken to an impressive tent. At the

door stood the most beautiful woman Melvyn had ever set eyes on, and yet she seemed totally unaware of her outward appearance. Her expressive eyes were full of laughter, as she took Melvyn by the hand and led him to a seat under some huge oak trees nearby.

"I will appear to you later," Immanuel told Melvyn.

"I am to tell you the story of God's choice of me to become the mother of his Covenant people. It's a pretty sad story at times but a funny one too. I became the wife of Abraham, my half-brother. We loved each other and he was very good to me but we had no children, which was a great sadness to me. The strange thing was that God had promised Abraham that his descendants would be too many to count. Years went by but still I had no children. I began to think that the children Abraham was to have must be by another woman, as I was obviously barren. I took matters into my own hands and asked Abraham to sleep with my slave-maid Hagar. I would then adopt her child as my own. God was not too thrilled by that course of action and I paid dearly for my lack of faith. Ishmael was born to Hagar and Abraham loved him, but thirteen years later God again promised Abraham a son by me. By that time I was well past menopause, and Abraham laughed to himself, he told me later.

The Covenant God made with us that day was to be sealed by male circumcision. Abraham lost no time and that very day he and Ishmael and all the males in our household, were circumcised.

Not long afterwards we had three special visitors. Abraham treated them with great respect, and together we prepared a feast for them. After they had eaten, I was listening at the tent door and I heard one of them promise that I would have a son that year. I can tell you I thought that was pretty funny, and I could hardly keep from laughing out loud, but when the visitor asked me if I thought that was too hard for God to accomplish, fear gripped my heart and I lied. I excused the lie to myself because I had only laughed inside.

A year later I was not the only one laughing. Everyone who heard that ninety year old Sarah had just had a son laughed too. We called our precious son Laughter. God was going to do a great work through Isaac, our miracle boy."

"Abraham had other sons. There was the boy Ishmael by your slave Hagar, and all the sons by his second wife Keturah, not to mention all his concubines' sons," Melvyn interrupted. "Why was your son so singled out?"

"He was the son of a promise. God was teaching Abraham and me and all generations after us, that he never breaks his promises. He made this an everlasting Covenant with Abraham. Isaac was the beginning of the fulfilment of God's pledge that through our descendants, all the nations of the earth would be blessed.

Perhaps God was also reminding us that his intention for marriage was monogamy. The Fall and sin brought in bigamy and concubines. Abraham indeed had many other children but the blessing for humanity came through my only son, Isaac. I was Abraham's only true wife at the time," Sarah explained.

"Why do you think God at a later date tested Abraham's love for Isaac as compared to Abraham's love for God? After all, if God knows everything, he must have known Abraham loved God more than anyone," Melvyn asked Sarah.

"True, Melvyn, but we had so much to learn and still do. God had to give us living parables and picture language to help us understand the coming of his own Son. Abraham loved my only son with true fatherly love. He was the apple of his eye. To be asked to sacrifice his most precious son was the hardest thing that anyone could ask of Abraham. Yet, in that potential sacrifice, Abraham saw something of what it cost our Heavenly Father to give his only Son to be sacrificed for the sins of the world. A substitute was provided at that time, in the form of a ram, but that was again only a picture of the reality that was provided in Christ. We could not but love our God more than ever, when we understood this true sacrifice.

Oh, look! There's my grandson, Israel," Sarah said pointing to an approaching figure.

"How is my beautiful grandmother?" Israel asked.

"Reminiscing with Melvyn here about my life with Abraham, and the birth of your dad," Sarah replied. "You can tell Melvyn some more about God's Covenant pledge to our family."

"I can certainly do that, Grandma," Israel said turning to Melvyn.

Melvyn said bye to Sarah who headed towards a sumptuously decked camel.

"Sarah still prefers camel transport. That's my grandma," Israel chuckled.

"What a very beautiful woman she is," Melvyn remarked as they both waved Sarah on her way.

"Oh, you haven't seen my Rachel," Israel protested.

"She can't be more beautiful than Sarah," Melvyn argued.

"Perhaps not, but she is very lovely and I was besotted with her from the first time I saw her."

"Then it must have been a shock when you woke up to find Leah in your wedding bed instead of Rachel"

"I don't want to talk about it. Some would say it was poetic justice, since I had tricked Esau out of his inheritance and my father's blessing. My father in law, Leban, and I were quite alike in that respect, and perhaps my mother Rebecca too, come to think of it. We were all devious. It must have been in the genes." They both laughed.

"Sarah has been telling me how God used living parables and picture language to teach people of your time about his plan to save the world. There was no written Bible until much later in history, of course."

"No, Moses, a descendent of mine through my son Levi, was the first to put in writing God's creation plans and dealings with us. Before that, we had to rely on history being passed down orally from one generation to the next."

"What did God teach you, Israel?"

"Well, for a start, that he can use and change even a rogue like me. Perhaps God's love and mercy are shown more clearly in operation, when the character has little to commend him. He cares for each of us and he is not far from any one of us. He showed me in a lonely desert place, with only a stone for a pillow, that heaven and earth are very closely linked if only we have eyes to see. His Son, Immanuel, is like the ladder I saw in my dream, connecting heaven and earth. He is the one who is both God and man, and as such he is the only mediator. He is the only one who understands both the human and the divine states. Through me God continued to fulfil his

Covenant pledge to Abraham. I became the father of the twelve tribes of Israel. My name, or rather the new name God gave me, became the name by which the Covenant partners of God were thereafter to be known – the Israelites."

"I see you're not limping anymore," Melvyn joked.

"Immanuel makes everything new," Israel replied patting his thigh. "I'll be seeing you, Melvyn. Bye!"

From the distance Melvyn noticed a couple of lovers approaching. The woman was leaning on the man and there was something familiar about her.

"Who is this I see coming up from the desert, arm in arm with her lover?" Melvyn asked but Israel was out of earshot. The lovers approached and Melvyn recognized Immanuel. He smiled at Melvyn. The woman's eyes were fixed on Immanuel; she did not seem to see Melvyn. Melvyn gasped when he recognised the woman.

It was Stella. Not Stella as she had been when he divorced her. She was young again, and even more beautiful than he remembered. Her dark eyes and hair were set off by her luminous skin. As he watched she caught up Immanuel's hands, kissed his scars and leaned her head against his side. Love oozed from every pore of her being as Immanuel wrapped her in his arms, and kissed her on the mouth. His terms of endearment embarrassed Melvyn. Immanuel looked at him, but said nothing.

In shame and confusion Melvyn blurted out: "I know! I know! I'm sorry. I didn't treat her well. I deprived her of my love and abused her cruelly with my tongue."

A rustling in the leaves and a still small voice distracted Melvyn:

"God was there as a witness when you spoke your marriage vows to your young bride, and now you've broken those vows, broken the faith-bond with your vowed companion, your covenant wife. GOD, not you, made marriage. His Spirit inhabits even the smallest details of marriage. And what does he want from marriage? Children of God, that's what. I hate divorce."

Melvyn sat down and put his head in his hands. What a mess he had made of his life. He got up and wandered off aimlessly. He got lost in a thick forest. A voice he recognized called his name: "Melvyn, what are you doing here?"

"I am sick at the way I messed up my life. I am a fool!"

"Melvyn, since you did not choose to make use of my love to love the wife I gave you, your love being only self-love, soon turned sour. Only in me could you love anyone as I love Stella. I love her so completely that every atom of her being comes alive in my arms. She has tasted real love, and from now on no substitute will satisfy her. She is mine and I am hers forever. I love her completely."

Melvyn sighed deeply, "What about Angelina? She no longer loves me. It all seems so hopeless and too late for change."

"It is never too late to love with my love," Immanuel answered gently, "but loving with my love is not easy. My love is costly and is not always reciprocated."

"I suppose Stella can never forgive me," Melvyn mused.

"Stella forgave you a long time ago. In me she has found true freedom that will never be taken away from her, and that includes forgiveness for those who have wronged her. Her life is free from bitterness and she is safe in my love. Come let's go!"

Big soft fluffy flakes of snow began to fall on Melvyn and Immanuel as they left the forest. In the distance they could hear sleigh bells, and the high pitched voices of children having fun. Soon they were joined by a group of children, who shyly crowded around Immanuel and smiled up at him.

"And what are you all up to?" Immanuel asked. "Surely we don't have to walk all the way to camp?" They scampered off.

In no time at all, a tall slim girl with fine blue eyes was back, with a team of equally blue-eyed huskies, pulling a red and silver sledge at great speed.

"Carrie, you've really got the hang of controlling those dogs now," Immanuel praised her. "Can I have a ride?"

"Of course! That's why I came. I'd love to give you a ride and Melvyn too," Carrie smiled. "We'll go the long way!"

Melvyn wondered how she knew his name.

They all got on the sled, and with a "Mush!" from Carrie they were off. The dogs behaved beautifully under the guidance of their gentle mistress. Even the long way was not far, and in no time they came to an igloo camp near a frozen lake. Children, dogs, reindeer, horses, penguins, bears and a medley of other animals were having the fun of their lives. Holes had been cut in the lake and several children were fishing. Snowmen were being built, another igloo was being constructed, sleds were flying down a snowy slope, and snowballs had to be dodged. Lista, a talented young ice skater, was pirouetting and performing with her friends, for her baby brother.

Nearby on a charcoal grill, Carrie's twin brother, Caspian, was cooking some fish he had caught. The smell was delicious and Melvyn, Immanuel, and lots of Caspian's friends were soon tucking in together.

The children all seemed to be full of life and energy. They seemed to be looking out for each other, and having fun was obviously the order of the day. No-one was left out. Some angels had charge over the children to keep them from getting hurt, but mostly to teach them skills, or to give them help harnessing and feeding the animals. Melvyn liked small children and thoroughly enjoyed his time with them.

Chapter Six

The Plan Unfolds

Later a small helicopter dropped down not far from the camp, creating a mini blizzard. Immanuel led Melvyn inside and they were off. They were taken to the base of a mountain, where a large tent with a long forecourt had been erected. People were milling about looking at tapestries hung from poles on all sides. Melvyn examined the first one and saw it depicted a baby in a basket being presented to an Egyptian princess. The basket was dripping water, and a young girl was spying on the scene from a hiding place among the long reeds on the river bank.

"Now, that's a beautiful baby if ever I saw one," came a voice from behind them.

"I had to make sure of that, Moses, or you might have been thrown right back into the Nile, as soon as you were taken out of it," Immanuel quipped back.

Melvyn looked at Moses, handsome baby, handsome man.

Moses turned to Melvyn, "Earlier, I believe you saw the largest floating ark ever built and now you see the smallest."

"Melvyn, this is where our plan for humanity took a great leap forward," Immanuel explained. "Moses was brought up as the princess' son and educated in all the wisdom of the Egyptians, but he was also familiar with the history of his own people the Hebrews, or Israelites. From the Egyptians he learned to read and write, and this skill was put to good use when it came to writing down the first Hebrew Scriptures. Until that time, the only accounts of the beginning of creation, and our dealings with humanity were passed down orally from one generation to the next."

"My parents made sure that I learned about the God of my ancestors, and the history of my people. Of course, I had to learn about the numerous Egyptian deities also, and their onerous demands on mankind."

"The Hebrew people were the descendants I had promised Abraham and Sarah years before, but by Moses' time they had been reduced to slavery, as predicted in the Covenant. We had not forgotten the Covenant we made with their forefathers Abraham, Isaac, and Jacob. In their slavery, redemption, desert wanderings, receiving of the Torah and other things, they were being taught in picture language and through events to trust God, and believe in his Covenant faith-fulness. Our plan for their redemption, and the renewal of the whole world through them, was to unfold in Hebrew history. Moses will explain it all to you."

"I can certainly try," Moses replied, "but good, here comes Priscilla. She's an authority on the Book of Hebrews, and much more articulate than I."

Immanuel was walking away shaking his head and saying, "Moses, Moses, you still think everyone can pontificate better than you."

Moses introduced Melvyn to Priscilla.

"Hi, Melvyn, I'm pleased to meet you!" Priscilla smiled.

"Hi, Priscilla, likewise," Melvyn replied with a nod.

Moses led the way over to the second tapestry. It depicted the cruel slavery endured by the Hebrews, and Moses and Aaron trying to reason with Pharaoh, while his plague-ridden, beleaguered subjects looked on helplessly.

"Our God had not forgotten his Covenant promises to Abraham, but to us their fulfilment seemed a long time in coming, and it certainly was a painful process," Moses sighed.

Priscilla added, "Yes, it took a long time for our nation to acquire the language and concepts needed to understand the role of the Messiah. We had to learn the necessity of his incarnation, life, death and resurrection for us. God did try in various ways at various times, through prophets and others, to explain what he was doing but really until Messiah came and lived as one of us, died and rose again, we had only the vaguest notion of his plan. When Messiah came he showed us what God, the Father, is really like. We were so mixed up we could not comprehend his love for all humanity and his creation. We thought he had chosen us alone to be his people, and that he regarded the rest of humanity as just promiscuous idolaters, as we did."

"I'm afraid we got so caught up in our special relationship with God that we forgot the purpose of that relationship," Moses added. "Yet God had made it clear to Abraham, and later to my generation, that we were to be a nation of priests that were to bring light to the Gentiles. We selfishly kept our light to ourselves. God's good plan was for all humanity to be redeemed, from the power and consequences of sin, and to be brought into the glorious liberty of the children of God. His purpose was the adoption of all humanity into the triune circle, through union with his beloved Son."

"We still find it hard to understand God's love for all he has made. We know it is huge and high and deep. It's like the ocean which is so vast we can't take in its dimensions, but we can dip a toe in it, we can swim in it, and we can enjoy it," Priscilla explained.

"Let's get an overview of all the tapestries and then we can listen to Priscilla explain the symbolism, using the Book of Hebrews in particular," Moses suggested.

The next tapestry showed the Passover and the Egyptians weeping over their dead firstborns. Moses repeated God's warning to Pharaoh, when he first refused to let the Hebrews go, "GOD's Message: Israel is my son, my firstborn! I told you, 'Free my son so that he can serve me.' But you refused to free him. So now I'm going to kill *your* son, *your* firstborn."

Moses continued sadly, "Time after time Pharaoh was warned with increasingly severe plagues, that God is not to be trifled with. The plagues he sent showed up the Egyptian gods as helpless to defend their worshipers. The god of the Nile, the god of the flies, the god of the frogs, and all the others were shown up as imposters who could not control their so-called domains. Until his firstborn was dead, Pharoah broke promise after promise to me.

That night we killed the Passover lambs, as instructed by God, and we had to sprinkle the blood of the sacrificed lambs on the door posts of each of our houses. The blood signified the life and death of the lamb, until the time came, when the true Lamb of God was sacrificed. We were protected that night from the angel of death, by the sign of that blood. Inside our houses, we ate the roasted lambs. Though we did not understand the full significance of the ritual, we were obedient. Anyway, by morning we and all our herds had been driven out of Egypt into the desert, towards the Red Sea. God had redeemed his people from slavery. Redemption was a concept God wanted to burn into our consciousness, to help us understand his plan."

"A picture of being bought or escaping from slavery to sin, I suppose?" Melvyn asked.

"That's right!" Moses replied moving on to the next tapestry. It depicted the crossing of the Red Sea.

"Here we see a picture of the baptism of our people going through the deadly water, safe in our God, and starting our new life in him. How happy we were that day, and how amazed at God's redemption of us from slavery. It was almost too good to be true.

My sister Miriam was a prophetess and a great singer and dancer too. She and I led the people in glorious worship that day. What a day it was. Free at last, free at last!"

The next tapestry depicted the quails, manna, and the water from the rock. Moses explained, "The Lord at that time also gifted us a Sabbath rest every seven days. You can imagine what that felt like to a former nation of slaves. The message was driven home by the provision of manna every day except on the Sabbath. We were instructed to gather double the amount of manna on the sixth day so that we could all rest on the seventh day. Our Lord later identified with the manna saying he was the true bread that came down from heaven, and also with the water from the rock, saying he was the living water that would quench the thirst of his people forever. He is the one who would give his people a true and lasting Sabbath rest, in the true land flowing with milk and honey, which is his own new kingdom."

In a self-explanatory tapestry, an appalled Moses was shown breaking the stone tablets written by God. Moses had gone up Mt. Sinai, at God's request, to be given the stone tablets. Over the forty days he was gone from the camp, the people grew restless. They grumbled to Aaron that Moses was gone, and as nobody knew what had happened to him, they should make themselves other gods to lead them. On the tapestry, Aaron was depicted by an altar with the golden calf he had made for the people. The people themselves were worshipping the golden calf, and dancing in wild idolatrous orgies and pagan rites, around the altar. Before the Law could even be read to them, they had already broken faith with God, but he forgave them.

Moving on they came to a tapestry that was mostly writing. Moses was depicted at the foot of Mt. Sinai reading the words from Exodus 19:

"You have seen what I did to Egypt and how I carried you on eagles' wings and brought you to me. If you will listen obediently to what I say and keep my covenant, out of all people you'll be my special treasure. The whole earth is mine to choose from, but you're special: a kingdom of priests, a holy nation."

The people were unanimous in their response: "Everything God says, we will do."

Next came tapestries of the giving of the Torah, the Law, but Moses told Melvyn that Paul the Apostle was the one who could best explain the purpose of the Torah to him. Moses was seen writing down all that the Lord had said, and the writings were known by names such as the Torah, the Law, and Book of the Covenant.

Paul was introduced to Melvyn, and then he explained that later the entire book of the Law was read to the people, and Moses sprinkled the people with the blood of the animals sacrificed the same day, as a sign that they were dead to sin and alive to God.

The Torah, Paul explained, was given as a type of babysitter to keep the elect nation of Israel in line, until the coming of Messiah. They badly misunderstood the teaching purposes of the Torah, and thought that through keeping Torah they would gain a place in the Messiah's kingdom. They did not understand that only the Messiah would be able to keep Torah perfectly, while also becoming the atoning sacrifice pictured in the rituals of the Tabernacle. Before his conversion he, Paul himself, had been an outwardly faultless, zealous keeper of the Torah. However, like every other ordinary human being, he could not live up to its inward demands for a sinless loving relationship with God and his neighbours. Only when Immanuel met him on the road to Damascus, to murder and imprison Christians, did he realize that the Torah had served its purpose. Up until that time he had not recognized the Messiah, or the truth that Messiah had fulfilled the Torah for his people, and had become the one faithful Israelite who fulfilled the Covenant and brought light to the world.

Paul further explained that since those who could not keep the Torah perfectly were under sentence of death, by dying Messiah ensured that the hold of the Torah over humanity was fulfilled and thus broken forever. Dead humans cannot be judged and condemned. In solidarity with Immanuel, humanity died, and the curse of the Torah was rendered obsolete. The babysitter had done her job, and she now had to release humanity back to its Saviour to be resurrected, and recreated, in him.

They had scarcely completed an overview of the tapestries when the blast of a silver trumpet was heard outside. Some people left while others seated themselves on cushions and rugs brought in by angels, who also removed the tapestries to reveal walls of blue, purple, and scarlet curtains, worked through with pictures of cherubim.

Priscilla was to take the role of guide in the proceedings that followed. When all was quiet, she pointed out the divisions of the tabernacle, the courtyard where the faithful gathered for prayer while the priests performed their duties, with the great sacrificial altar at one end and huge wash basins for serving priests at the other end. The audience was sitting in the Holy Place, she explained, which would have been completely empty except for the High Priest on an actual Day of Atonement, which was now to be re-enacted.

At the far end of the Holy Place, was the heavy embroidered curtain separating it from the Holy of Holies, which housed the golden Ark of the Covenant. The ark contained the stone tablets on which were written the Ten Commandments, and also Aaron's rod and a jar of manna. The pure gold lid of the ark was called the mercy seat, or atonement seat. At each end of the seat were hammered gold cherubim facing each other, and looking down at the seat with their wings spreading above the seat. A copy of the complete Torah was placed beside the ark.

There too stood the golden altar of incense. Just outside the dividing curtain the light of the golden lamp stand, with its decorative branches of almond buds and blossoms, cast its beautiful glow on the gold plated table with its plates, dishes, bowls, and pitchers of pure gold for drink offerings. There were no windows in the tabernacle; it was lit only by the lamps. The most Holy Place was lit once a year by the smoky censor of coals and incense carried in by the High Priest during his duties. He would die if he saw the glory of God over the mercy seat. The cloud of incense prevented him from seeing the glory of God.

Actors arrived dressed in magnificent priestly robes. Priscilla explained the significance of the High Priest's garments, especially the gold, blue, purple and scarlet ephod, with its shoulder pieces of onyx stones set in gold filigree and engraved with the names of Israel's twelve sons. The golden breastplate, mounted with four rows of three precious stones each, was also engraved with the names of the twelve tribes of Israel and attached to the ephod and waistband with gold rings and blue cords. On the bottom of the robe, which was all blue and woven in one piece, were embroidered pomegranates alternating with pure gold bells. Attached to the High Priest's turban with blue cord was a gold plate, engraved with the words, "Holy to the Lord."

"The High Priest symbolically taking all Israel with him on his shoulders and over his heart, in a tabernacle like this, went right into the Holy of Holies once a year, on the Day of Atonement. He always had to take blood with him to make atonement for his own sins and for the sins of the people.

For himself and his family he had to offer a bull. For the people he had to offer a goat from a pair of goats. One of the goats was chosen by lot to be killed, and the other one had to become a scapegoat. The blood of the bull and goat were taken by the high priest, who had to be washed and clothed in his ceremonial garments, into the Holy of Holies.

His first duty was to take burning coals from the altar sprinkled with two handfuls of incense into the Holy of Holies to hide the mercy seat from being seen by him. He then had to take some blood on his finger and sprinkle the front of the mercy seat once. Then near its base he had to sprinkle blood seven times. Afterwards he had to go out of the Holy of Holies, dress in his normal clothes in the Holy place, and proceed to the great altar where he laid both his hands on the head of the live scapegoat, confessing the sins of all the people. The sins of the people were symbolically transferred onto the goat, and the goat was taken far out into the wilderness and set free. Meanwhile the body of the bull and the other goat were completely burned in some place outside the camp.

Two rams were offered on the altar by the high priest as burnt offerings, one for the priest and his family, and one for the people. These rituals were, of course, only pictures that pointed to the day when the great High Priest, Messiah the Son of God, would have the sin of the world gathered up on his head to be carried away forever through his death and burial. He would go through to the real Holy of Holies for us, offering his own body and lifeblood for us, before sitting down as our mediator to make constant intercession for us. All these rituals were to teach us to recognize the true High Priest and mediator when he came," Priscilla explained.

She continued, "The Book of Hebrews explains to us that Jesus is the Son of God, who became a true human while remaining true God. As such, he is able to sympathize with our weaknesses and temptations. He himself resisted all temptation but at a cost. To be at all times in a right relationship with the Father through the Spirit, his life was one of suffering and struggle to resist sin and remain obedient to his Father's will. He had to war against weak flesh. His flesh from Mary was the only human flesh around at that time, and it was fallen human flesh. To heal the human mind and fallen human flesh he had to take on both, without succumbing to sin. With perseverance he lived and offered that spotless life we could never achieve, in full obedience to the Father. He alone of all humanity lived loving God with all his heart, soul, mind and strength. In human weakness he lived dependent on the Holy Spirit.

The earthly High Priests and the other priests offered various sacrifices daily as the Torah prescribed. On the Day of Atonement the high priests had to offer blood sacrifices year after year, first for their own sins and then for the sins of the people. Jesus offered his own blood, his lifeblood in his death, once for all for the sins of all humanity. He was the true High Priest, not a shadow high priest like Aaron and subsequent high priests. He entered into the real Holy of Holies in heaven, not the shadow copy of the Holy of Holies to be found on earth.

As with almost all the elements found in the tabernacle, the curtain concealing the earthly Holy of

Holies was a symbol. It was a symbol of Christ's body, and this shadow curtain, not surprisingly, was supernaturally ripped from top to bottom the instant Christ gave up his life. Christ did not bring a breastplate of jewelled names, an external symbol of the people, into the true Holy of Holies in heaven. He brought humanity, in union with himself, from slavery to sin through death to eternal redemption. The new exodus complete, he sat down with them in heaven where his very being, still human and still divine, makes intercession for us forever. Such is the unchanging character of our God and his eternal plan for rescuing us from all the consequences of our Fall into sin. In union with Christ, we are accepted as Christ is accepted, and are as such God's children.

The Old Covenant was thus fulfilled in Christ, and has now been replaced by reality. That does not mean it was a bad thing. It fulfilled its purpose; it taught those willing to learn from its elements, rituals, and liturgy, and is no longer needed. The real has replaced the symbol. The New Covenant in Christ's blood is now in force and is written on our hearts, not on tablets of stone."

Miriam, followed by a band of dancers, came in at that point singing:

"May God, who puts all things together,
makes all things whole,
Who made a lasting mark through the sacrifice of
Jesus,
the sacrifice of blood that sealed the eternal covenant,
Who led Jesus, our Great Shepherd,
up and alive from the dead,

Now put you together, provide you
with everything you need to please him,
Make us into what gives him most pleasure,
by means of the sacrifice of Jesus, the Messiah.
All glory to Jesus forever and always!
Oh, yes, yes, yes."

Without warning the curtain to the Holy of Holies was ripped open and there on the atonement seat sat Immanuel, clothed in dazzling brilliance. Awe gripped every heart and people instinctively shielded their eyes, and fell prostrate before him, as cherubim appeared singing, "Holy, holy, holy," with wings covering their faces.

As suddenly as it had appeared the vision disappeared, and once again the shadow tabernacle went quiet and people got up and started leaving. The angels began replacing the tapestries and removing the rugs. All was being put in order again for further viewing.

Chapter Seven

Reflections and a Meeting with Joshua

Melvyn had been thrown completely off guard. Overwhelmed by the brilliance of the vision, fear had gripped his heart and he shook from head to foot. This was an aspect of God he had no ability to grasp.

Melvyn's father had been a preacher in a rather small conservative denomination. From early childhood Melvyn had heard the Bible read, and he had attended worship services in the church regularly. Though somewhat aloof, his father was considered a fine preacher, and for the most part his congregation seemed appreciative of his pastoral counsel and care of them. Melvyn he seldom praised, and often faulted in spite of Melvyn's tireless efforts to please him. Should Melvyn's examination results at school fall below one hundred per cent, even by as little as a point or two, his father was quick to reprimand him with a, "God is perfect and demands perfection. You must strive for one hundred per cent next time."

Any misdemeanour, even committed in ignorance, was treated with a harshness that would have surprised those who thought they knew him. Melvyn was often belted and banished to his room to contemplate his sinfulness, and beg God's forgiveness. His mother was of little support to him. She squashed his natural sense of humour, was eagle-eyed, judgemental, and critical of any high spirits, especially those displayed in front of the congregation.

"We must always be circumspect and a good witness to the congregation," she warned her little boy. When her husband treated Melvyn with a heavy hand she just shook her head, looked grave, and seemed to agree with this treatment of their son.

Melvyn, at one time, believed them when they told him they were punishing him for his own good. However, as time went on his spirit became surly. He obeyed outwardly, avoided trouble, kept himself to himself, ignored the criticisms levelled at him, and decided he wanted as little as possible to do with his parents and his parent's God, as he could get away with.

At college, away from home and parental restraint, little by little he cast off the taboos and restrictions of his childhood teachings. God did not seem bothered by his sins, and no bolt of lightning struck him. He seldom attended church, no longer read his Bible, and soon decided God was all pie in the sky nonsense. By his second year away from home he no longer believed in God, and he became quite arrogant in his interactions with those who did. As time went on he returned home less and less. He had nothing left in common with his parents; he even pitied them, despising what he saw as their lack of sophistication. His philosophy became live and let live, indulge oneself as long as it does not hurt others, try to be socially responsible, and help make the world a better place for everyone to live in. His new god was logic. He worshipped reason as defined by the Greek western mind, and the evidence of his eyes. He believed he was not ultimately influenced by emotion or instinct but only by facts, verifiable facts. Anything beyond the scope of his reason must be nonsense. He had no inkling that to use his reason, he had to rely on his learned and accepted pre-suppositions.

Still badly shaken, Melvyn followed the throng leaving the replica tabernacle. They did not seem to see him. They looked radiant, like happy newlyweds joyful and beyond speech. All of them had embraced the vision, and been thrilled by the experience. Melvyn had to find a place to be alone to process all this. He had hardly started walking away from the crowd when he found himself back beside the stream again.

"Is this a dream or is it real?" he shouted angrily to no one in particular. He stooped, cupped some water in his hands, and drank shakily. Sitting down on the grassy bank, his head between his knees and his hands clasped over the back of his head, he tried to think but his mind was blank. He stretched out on his back and let the gentle warmth soothe him. Soon he fell into a deep sleep. He dreamed Joshua came and sat beside him.

Still grumpy, he remembered the complete annihilation of the cities and towns, as Canaan was subdued and re-inhabited by the Hebrews, under Joshua's command.

"How in the world did you justify the slaughter of every man, woman, child, and animal, in the invasion of Canaan?" Melvyn challenged Joshua.

Joshua said nothing but led Melvyn up a high mountain ridge, and pointed to the towns and cities in the valleys below. With the aid of some binoculars Joshua handed him, Melvyn was able to zoom in and see close up, not only the cities and towns but the inhabitants and what they were up to. Invading armies were ransacking the cities. Murder, rape, pillage, torture, and kidnapping were the order of the day. Unbelievable cruelty was inflicted on the inhabitants of the towns and even on fellow soldiers, as they fought each other for the best houses, the most beautiful women, the best fields, the cattle, gold, jewellery and other plunder.

"This is what you did to gain the Promised Land?" Melvyn shouted aghast, handing back the binoculars. Joshua did not take them. He only said, "Look again!"

This time Melvyn saw a disciplined but determined army conquer city after city. The inhabitants were indeed wiped out but in comparison with what he had seen previously, the deaths were swift and humane. No one was tortured and no one was raped, and it was all over before anyone had time to mourn.

"I see," said Melvyn.

"There was one king, more depraved than any other we had come across. To him the tribe of Judah did give a taste of his own medicine," Joshua conceded, "but I was dead by that time."

"I don't remember." Melvyn inquired, "What was the incident?"

"King Adoni-Bezek was attacked by the tribe of Judah, who put the Canaanites and Perizzites to rout. Adoni-Bezek fled, but was caught and had his thumbs and big toes cut off."

"That's gross!" Melvyn gasped.

"Adoni-Bezek admitted what everyone else knew, 'Seventy kings with their thumbs and big toes cut off used to crawl under my table, scavenging. Now God has done to me what I did to them.'"

"What a butcher! It looks as if he got what he deserved," Melvyn conceded.

"Your sense of justice comes from God even if it is flawed. In this case God did not ask that Adoni-Bezek's thumbs and toes be cut off; the Bible only describes the violence done to him. The annihilation of the Canaanites was ordered by God and is a different matter altogether. God told Abraham that it would be several hundred years before his descendants would inherit Canaan because the wickedness of the Amorites had not yet reached a point of no return. By the time I was ordered to annihilate the people of Canaan their barbarity was beyond sadistic. God had been patient with the Canaanites for a very long time but their behaviour only got worse by the day. God was ready to avenge the victims. Vengeance belongs to God alone and he promises to repay the evildoers on behalf of the victims. God alone knows what is just in every circumstance and we simply obeyed his commands.

We see the same principle at work in the time of the kings when King Saul was asked to annihilate the wicked people, the Amalekites. King Saul, in defiance of God, spared the life of King Agag. Samuel would have none of it. Before killing King Agag Samuel told him, 'Just as your sword made many a woman childless, so your mother will be childless among those women!'

God sees the big picture, the whole of it even when we do not, and we can trust him to be merciful, patient and just always."

Suddenly Melvyn woke up and found he was alone again.

"I've been dreaming," he thought, "but wait, this is all a dream anyway. It must be a dream within a dream. I must be going crazy."

"I must be going crazy!" he repeated aloud. "What is real? I don't know what is real anymore!"

Again he closed his eyes but he could not keep his thoughts together. The gurgle of the water, and the soft warmth of the air on the grassy bank, soon lulled his tired brain back to sleep.

Images floated through his mind. Joshua was dead and the elders who outlived Joshua had died. Canaan, the Promised Land, was settled. Israelites were living in towns and cities they had not built, in houses they had not constructed. They were eating produce from fields they had not planted and from farms they had not cultivated. They were drinking wine from vineyards they had not established. Flocks and herds were thriving and families were living in peace and security. The Israelites were keeping God's Covenant. Morning and evening they showed their loving obedience by offering animal sacrifices, and their devotion by offering incense and prayer. They worshipped faithfully Sabbath by Sabbath and celebrated festivals joyfully, as the law required, and the priests instructed. They lived under the promised blessings of the Covenant, and God the Lord was their protector.

Melvyn stirred. He woke and drank again from the stream. He sat back in the grassy knoll. He knew he could go to the big house for breakfast but he was not hungry. He needed to think. Joshua flitted back into his mind, and the land of milk and honey where everyone had enough, and justice prevailed for all. It had not lasted long. He thought back to the Bible stories he had learned as a child. How soon the Israelites forgot that God had rescued them from slavery in Egypt. How soon they slipped back into paganism. They forgot the God of their fathers. Had not he, Melvyn, done the same? He no longer believed in God.

A voice from the rustling trees spoke into his heart, "Maybe, Melvyn, the god you forsook was a parody of the true God. Your parents presented you with a very imperfect picture of God. They coupled this with harsh treatment of you, which they passed off as God's will. The Father can only be known through his Son, Immanuel."

"I'm afraid of God," Melvyn admitted. "All that dazzling radiance is too much for me. I can't take it and I am afraid it will consume me."

"You have to be ready to be able to trust yourself to our consuming fire. What you do not realize is that it is a good fire. Everything that does not belong to the true human we created you to be, will be burned away. You will emerge from that fire whole, clean, beautiful inside and outside, full of holy love. The journey is long and hard. The journey is the fire. Now rise and eat and afterwards you will be shown what you must do."

There on a fiery rock was a sizzling quail and wafer bread spread with honey. How good it smelled. How wonderful it tasted washed down with fruit juice.

Joshua had long gone from his dreams and mind. A woman appeared with a pot of fresh coffee. He seemed to be in different surroundings. The stream was gone and he was sitting under a palm tree.

"I'm Hannah," she explained as she poured them both some coffee. "I am to show you more of the history of God's chosen people when you are ready. There's no rush."

Melvyn sucked in his breath, opened his eyes and murmured, "God is in this place – truly. And I didn't even know it."

"What?" came a familiar strident voice, "What did you say?"

"Nothing, Angelina, nothing," Melvyn replied. "Could I have some water?"

Angelina poured him a glass of water.

"Thanks! This is not up to the standard of the new world water but it will have to do," Melvyn told her between sips.

"What are you talking about? What new world water?"

"Nothing! Nothing at all! Just a dream, I think a dream."

Angelina grunted and said accusingly, "You need to get a grip!"

Melvyn closed his eyes for a moment. "I need to get a grip. Yes, I need to get a grip," he murmured exhausted, and closed his eyes.

Chapter Eight

Melvyn Meets the Judges and Kings

Melvyn savoured the steaming mug of coffee Hannah had poured for him, and she did the same with her own cup. He felt at peace. People were arriving from the surrounding hills and valleys. They introduced themselves and sat down under the palms, drinking coffee and chatting. At last Hannah opened proceedings.

"Melvyn, you know that after Joshua died the Israelites embraced paganism. Part of the Covenant decreed that if the Israelites did that, God would abandon them to their enemies and to the curses of the Covenant. Sadly that happened many times on a small scale.

I've gathered together the judges that God raised up to bring Israel back to himself and to liberation from their enemies. Judge after judge defended, ruled, and led the people back to Covenant faithfulness. Sadly time after time when the judge died, the Israelites were seduced into worshipping idol gods once more. We want you to know how faithful and loyal God is. He continued to keep his promises, even when he was provoked repeatedly, by our faithlessness and disobedience. He chose to rescue, bless and teach us over and over again. We certainly were not becoming the light of the world as we were expected to become.

Still, God will not have his good creation and creatures ruined and brought to chaos. God is love and wants the best for all of us. He wants us to live in reality and truth, secure and safe in his protection. The foolish deceptions of idolatry lead only to lies, fear, injustice, hatred, and cruelty, which anger him. He will not put up with the weak being exploited.

Here are the judges that God used to rescue Israel, when God reluctantly withdrew his protection from Israel, and allowed the curses of the Covenant to take effect. The curses were as much a part of the Covenant as the blessings. Faithless Israel was plundered, defeated in battle, and subjected to paying crippling tributes to alien kings. However, as our God promised, when we turned back to God in our misery he would listen to us. He sent us judges to rescue and lead us back to his love again. He pitied us and was ever ready to hear our cries for help, when we turned back to him, after our dalliances with idolatry and wickedness. As long as we kept Covenant with God, we lived in security."

Hannah turned and pointed to a man close to her, "This is Othniel. He was a nephew of Caleb. Caleb and Joshua were the only two men who had lived in Egypt, who were allowed to enter Canaan, after the forty years of wandering in the desert. He first gained fame as a fighting man after Joshua died.

Later when the Israelites intermarried with the pagans in the surrounding areas (a practice they were continually warned against), they began worshipping the idol gods of these pagans. God then gave them over to the oppression of King Cushan-Rishathaim for eight years. Some Israelites became slaves and the rest virtual slaves. Eventually Israel began to listen to the remnant who still believed in God, and they began to pray to God in their misery. God was moved to pity for them in their groaning, and sent his Spirit on Othniel. Othniel defeated King Cushan-Rishathaim and Israel's oppressors, and went on to rule Israel for forty years of happy prosperity, until his death.

"What happened then?" Melvyn asked.

"Need you ask?" Ehud responded. "Back Israel went to wickedness of every kind. King Eglon of Moab, in alliance with the Ammonites and Amalekites, defeated Israel. Again we were badly oppressed and made to pay heavy taxes to Eglon."

"I remember now," Melvyn laughed. "You were the one who hid a long double-edged sword under your clothes. Eglon was a very fat king, and you were the one who brought him the taxes from Israel. You assassinated King Eglon."

"Yes, he trusted me, and nobody expected me to be carrying a concealed sword on my right side; they didn't know I was left handed. When I told Eglon I had a secret message for him, he sent all his attendants out of his rooftop room, and received me alone. He was so fat that not only the blade but the hilt of the sword disappeared into his flesh. I left it there and got out of the room as quickly as I could, locking the door behind me. Later his servants finding the door locked thought he wanted privacy. I was well on my way by the time they decided to investigate further, and force open the door. Once I got home I rallied the Israelites to war. We defeated Moab and we lived in peace under God's protection for a further eighty years."

"After Ehud, Shamgar delivered Israel," Hannah said pointing to him. "He once killed six hundred Philistines with an ox goad."

Shamgar smiled and said, "Yes, during Ehud's life the Moabites became subject to us, but the Philistines were becoming more and more troublesome for us. Then after I died, the Israelites once again returned to their evil ways and God let King Jabin of Canaan defeat us. We had to endure his cruelty for twenty years."

"I remember," Melvyn interrupted looking at a couple of women sitting under a palm. He forgot for a moment who was Deborah and who Jael. They both looked so noble there was no telling which was the judge, and which the brave assassin of the depraved commander, Sisera.

Guessing his thoughts Deborah spoke up, "I'm Deborah, the prophetess, and I was ruler of Israel for forty years. This is Barak, who I sent to battle at the Lord's command, but who refused to go unless I went along with him."

Barak looked at her admiringly, "I didn't have your faith, Deborah, but what a victory God gave us that day. I believed then, and I sang, and rejoiced, and worshipped after that amazing victory."

Deborah turned to Jael, "Melvyn do you remember the part Jael played in our victory?"

"I do indeed," Melvyn smiled and began reciting from the Book of Judges:

'most blessed of all women is Jael,
wife of Heber the Kenite,
most blessed of homemaking women.'

Sisera came to your tent to hide. What a brave thing you did. Were you not afraid Sisera would wake up and kill you?"

"The Lord gave me courage and strength," Jael admitted humbly. "To do his will is my delight." Her eyes glowed with inward peace, "Barak did the hard work."

"I could hardly believe my eyes when you showed me into your tent," Barak added. "I knew then it was all over for King Jabin, though it took a while longer and hard fighting to finish the task."

"But history kept repeating itself," Melvyn reflected. "Once Deborah died the people slid back into idolatry, depravity, and degradation, did they not?"

"Indeed they did, and for eight years they were plundered and killed by the Midianites. Their only respite was hiding in the mountain caves," Hannah continued. "Now meet Gideon who has an interesting story to tell."

"'God is with you, O mighty warrior,' if I remember correctly," Melvyn laughed. "I don't think you believed that at the time, Gideon?"

"No, I wasn't of much significance as the youngest member of my family. At the time the angel hailed me I was hiding in the wine press threshing corn, so that the Midianites wouldn't find it and steal it."

"But you did believe in God. You knew the history of your people?"

"Oh yes, but my family also sacrificed to Baal and other pagan deities. What a mess we were in. We hedged our bets by worshipping different gods. It wasn't only what the Midianites would do to me I was afraid of but also what my own family and townspeople would do to me, if I insulted Baal by desecrating his altar, as the angel told me to do."

"You did obey though?"

"Yes, I desecrated Baal's altar and the sacred pole beside it. That night (I didn't dare do these things in the daytime) I built an altar to the Lord as instructed. I then sacrificed one of my father's bulls on it using a sacred Asherah pole as kindling. After that I waited for the storm to break in the morning."

"It seems your father was pretty astute in defending you against the townspeople?"

"Oh, yes! When they wanted to kill me, he told them that Baal was not much of a god if he couldn't defend himself."

"Yes," Melvyn agreed. "I never could fathom all the religious wars and persecutions that have occurred over the centuries, and even nowadays, to defend some god, or one religion or another. Only a wimp god can't defend himself."

"You're absolutely right. Baal didn't lift a finger to hurt me. Indeed I immediately rallied the troops for battle as instructed, though I was still fearful and pleaded with God to give me a sign that he would give us victory."

"Your famous wool fleeces, I believe?"

"Yes indeed but by that time, of course, it was all or nothing, trust God or die. I decided to trust God and to follow his instructions to the letter, even although it meant depleting my army from thirty-two thousand to three hundred men. With our three hundred men the

Midianites were put to flight. Then I called up the Israelites again to pursue and finish off the army of one hundred and thirty-five thousand.

This they did, but after the battle I did a stupid wicked thing. Ishmaelites wear gold earrings and these were plundered from the dead. I asked all the Israelite who had plundered from the enemy, to give me one earring each. They were glad to give them to me, and I made a gold ephod from them. In no time the Israelites began to worship the ephod. We did have peace for forty years in spite of this, but right after my death, the Israelites returned to full blown paganism, and my own family met a sorry end, killed by Abimelech, my son by a concubine. My sons had denied Abimelech any part of the inheritance when I died. He ruled for three years after my death, before he too came to a sorry end."

"Tola here brought the people back to their senses and he judged Israel for twenty-three years," Hannah continued when Gideon had finished speaking. "He was followed by Jair for twenty-two years, but after his death the Israelites again returned to paganism, and again fell under the curses of the Covenant. The Philistines and the Ammonites crushed and oppressed the Israelites cruelly for eighteen years. Finally our people repented, got rid of their idols, and started to serve the Lord only. The Lord then sent Jephthah, who defeated their enemies and ruled Israel for six years. After him Ibzan here ruled Israel for seven years, Elon for ten years, Abdon for eight years, and then back the Israelites went to their evil ways for forty years. Manoah will tell you the next part of our history."

"Well, my wife and I wanted children but sadly had none. Then one day the angel of the Lord appeared to my wife to tell her she was going to have a child who was to be a Nazarite, and that during her pregnancy she also was to observe the usual Nazarite dietary restrictions. This child was destined to become the deliverer of Israel from the Philistines, to whom we were subject at the time. I earnestly prayed God to send us his messenger again to teach us how to bring up the boy.

The angel again appeared to my wife and this time she ran to get me. When I asked for further directions, he just told me that my wife was to follow carefully the instructions he had already given her. I offered to prepare a young goat for him. He refused to eat but said the goat could be sacrificed as a burnt offering to the Lord. I did not know I was talking to the Lord even after he told me that his name (which I had asked for) was beyond understanding. I offered the goat and as the blazing flame of the burnt offering rose up, the angel of the Lord rose up on the flame. We fell on our faces to the ground and I was quite sure we were going to die there and then, since we had seen the Lord. However, my wife pointed out that if God wanted to kill us he would not have accepted our offering, nor would he have promised us such a special child. She was right, of course.

As our child grew up God's blessing was on him, and from time to time his Spirit anointed him. However as a gown-up he became quite a handful. First he wanted to marry a Philistine woman. We were not at all pleased as the Lord had often warned his people not to intermarry with pagans, as they would lead our children astray to worship idol gods. Samson (that's what we called him) was so determined to have the woman that we had no choice but to give in to him. Now we know that this was God's way of giving Samson a reason to confront the Philistines. Samson here can tell you the rest of his story."

"I think I know most of your story, Samson," Melvyn nodded towards him. "Mind you, I am curious as to what was going on in your head when you were chasing all those Philistine women."

Samson smiled, "You may well ask! The first I married, but I was angry when she tricked me. I set the Philistine wedding companions her family had given me a riddle, with a hefty prize for me if they could not solve it. The Philistines could not answer my riddle, but they threatened my new wife if she could not wheedle the answer out of me, for them. She told them the answer as soon as I gave it to her. I was obliged to find and kill a bunch of Philistines to get enough plunder to settle the agreement I had made with the wedding companions. I returned home in a huff without her.

Months later, realizing my new wife had little choice in the matter (my Philistine wedding companions had threatened to burn her and her father in their house, if she didn't get the answer out of me), I went back to consummate my marriage. It was then I found out she had been married off to my best man, as soon as I left. For revenge I burnt the wheat fields, olive groves, and the vineyards of the surrounding Philistines.

When they found out why I had done this, they burnt my wife and her father in their house anyway. I then killed a mass of them for burning my in-laws. That led to the Philistines invading Judah, already vassals to the Philistines, to give me up to them. I let the men of Judah tie me up and hand me over to the Philistines, but as soon as the Philistines rushed in to take me, the Spirit of the Lord came on me and I broke the ropes with ease.

With the jaw bone of an ass that was lying nearby, I killed a thousand men. That day I became judge of Israel and was judge for twenty years."

"What about the Gaza prostitute you visited?" Melvyn asked. "That got you into a spot of bother, did it not?"

"Yes, but again God saved me. The people of Gaza found out where I was, so they locked the city gates hoping to capture me at first light, and kill me. I left in the night by lifting the city gates, carrying them off posts and all, and escaping well before dawn."

"Amazing!" Melvyn admitted. "But worse was to come. You fell in love with Delilah. People reading your story down the centuries are baffled by the fact that three times Delilah betrayed you to the Philistines, and yet you went on to tell her the secret of your great strength. You must have known she would cut your hair and betray you again? What were you thinking?"

"I was besotted with Delilah, completely under her spell. Sensually she was beyond compare, satisfying my every whim, even ones I didn't know I had. She knew every trick and she played me until I became completely addicted to her, and couldn't give her up."

"But you must have known that you would be in grave danger if you told your secret to her. Why did you give in and tell her?"

"I believe your generation calls it self-deception or being in denial. I was Delilah's slave. I couldn't give her up. I had married a Philistine woman against God's law and my parents' wishes, and yet God had saved me from the consequences. I had been with a prostitute in Gaza, again flying in the face of God's law, but yet God had saved me at that time too. God would save me from

Delilah's treachery because I was special, and God would give me extraordinary strength every time I needed it to defeat the Philistines. What pride, what foolishness, and how little I knew the Lord. How terribly I paid for my blind wickedness. The Philistines gouged out my eyes and I was shackled in bronze, and made to work like an ox going round and round grinding corn, in the prison mill.

Blind, weak, humiliated, and relentlessly mocked, my hair began to grow in prison, and with it my strength began to return. The Philistines, feeling secure in their superiority over Israel, decided to have a great festival to honour their god Dagon for delivering me into their hands. They arranged a huge celebration in Dagon's temple, attended by thousands, and I was brought out of prison to entertain the crowd. You know the story. I asked the attendant who led me out of prison to place me between the two main pillars on which the temple rested. I felt with my hands and I prayed earnestly to God for the strength to dislodge the pillars. That day I died, as I knew I would if God answered my prayer, but more Philistines died with me that day, than I had killed during my entire lifetime. Thousands inside were crushed, and thousands on the rooftop tumbled to their deaths. Now you know."

"Now I know," Melvyn reflected.

After a pause for more coffee and chit chat, Hannah resumed, "Now comes the story of Eli and Samuel, my wonderful son from God. I first met Eli, the priest and judge at the time, when I was praying in the tabernacle court in great distress. You probably cannot begin to imagine the constant insinuations, mockery and disgrace heaped on a barren wife, in my day. My husband's other wife, Peninnah, was the worst of all. She knew my husband loved me more than her, but she had loads of children and people regarded her as blessed, and me as cursed. She never gave me a moment's peace, especially if she overheard Elkanah tell me, as he often did when I was downcast, that he loved me and treated me better than ten sons could.

Anyway, one particular year when we went up for the annual sacrifice at the tabernacle, and Peninnah was being even more vicious than usual, I couldn't even eat. I went instead to the tabernacle to pray. I prayed in my heart but my lips were moving, and my face may well have been contorted by intense emotion. Eli was sitting not far from me, and he thought I was drunk and chided me. When he realized his mistake he was very kind, and prayed that God would grant me my request.

God did indeed grant me my heart's desire. I had made a promise when I was praying, that I would give the child to the Lord's service for life, if he answered me. Because of the promise, I declined to redeem my firstborn as the Torah demanded of non Levites, and instead I dedicated him to the Lord's service forever.

When he was old enough I took him up to Eli to start his training in the tabernacle. Every year after that, I took him a set of clothes as he outgrew his old ones. I also introduced him to his new brothers and sisters, as God blessed me with more children. Samuel was a wonderful child, who very early learned to love and serve the Lord. Indeed it was not long before everyone realized that God had chosen Samuel to become a prophet and leader of his people.

After the tragic death of Eli and his sons, Samuel became Israel's judge. I'm afraid that just as Eli's sons

did not follow in their father's footsteps, Samuel's sons did not follow his example either. For whatever reason, the people began pestering Samuel to anoint them a king to lead them in battle, just as the kings of the other nations around them. Samuel will give you an overview of the next part of our history and how it fitted into God's plan for humanity. You'll find him in the portrait gallery of the kings of Israel and Judah. I'll take you there."

Hannah left Melvyn inside the portrait gallery, assuring him that Samuel would soon arrive. The gallery was a replica of the Palace of the Forest of Lebanon. It was very grand and smelled wonderful, since it was built mainly of cedar wood. The building was supported by four rows of massive cedar columns, supporting massive cedar beams that in turn held up a roof of cedar. The windows were set high in the walls, in sets of three facing each other on opposite walls. All the doorways had rectangular frames. One end of the building had a colonnade and portico with pillars, and an overhanging roof. Further on in exact replica was the throne room, and the living quarters Solomon had built for himself, plus other living quarters built for Pharoah's daughter, who had become one of his wives.

Many of the portraits were executed in stained glass, throwing patterns of glowing colours on the floor below. Both Israel's and Judah's kings were depicted. Under each portrait a caption denoted those who did what was right in the eyes of the Lord, and those who did what was evil in the eyes of the Lord. Down the centre of the gallery and along walls were displays of artefacts and things of significance, in the lives of the various kings.

An imposing full size wax replica of King Saul showed him in full armour, with his huge sword and shield.

Near King David's portrait lay his sling and Goliath's sword. His harp and copies of the Psalms he had written lay beside a magnificent gold bejewelled crown, which he had captured in one of his battles.

Many of Solomon's rich garments, his jewellery, his wives' jewellery, his attendant's costumes, gold and silver cups and plates, and other articles of great beauty and value in their time, were attractively displayed.

Melvyn looked around and sighed at this time capsule of Israel's kings from so long ago. He thought of the chequered lives of even the best of these men. Their ambitions, lust for power, for prestige, for wealth, their wisdom and foolishness, their kindness and cruelty, their wars and conquests were long gone. What did any of it matter anymore? He examined all the portraits and displays, and returned once more to the first kings, and the wax figure of Saul.

A gentle voice behind him startled him from his reverie.

"Melvyn, I warned them of the consequences of asking for a king, and the Lord had me spell it out for them:

'This is the way the kind of king you're talking about operates. He'll take your sons and make soldiers of them – chariotry, cavalry, infantry, regimented in battalions and squadrons. He'll put some to forced labor on his farms, plowing and harvesting, and others to making either weapons of war or chariots in which he can ride in luxury. He'll put your daughters to work as beauticians and waitresses and cooks. He'll conscript your best fields, vineyards, and orchards and hand them over to his special friends. He'll tax your harvests and vintage to support his extensive bureaucracy. Your prize workers and best animals he'll take for his own use. He'll lay a tax on your flocks and you'll end up no better than slaves. The day will come when you will cry in desperation because of this king you so much want for yourselves. But don't expect God to answer.'"

"Kings, judges – there seems to be little difference between them. What was the point? They each had a few years of glory or shame, and then they died. The times of the kings were as chequered as the times of the judges. I mean as far as keeping the Covenant was concerned, was it not?" Melvyn asked.

"In some ways, the times were much the same. The biggest difference was that in the times of the judges everyone did what was right in their own eyes, until the judges called them back to do what was right in God's eyes. With the kings everyone, or just about everyone, followed what was right in the king's eyes. If the king did what was right in the eyes of the Lord the people followed, and if the king did what was evil in the eyes of the Lord the people went along with that too. These were the days of the great prophets sent to call the kings and the people back to God. The prophets warned, cajoled, performed plays and set up concrete parables to remind the king and people, that if they persisted in breaking the Covenant, God in faithfulness to his side of the Covenant, had to send them death, slavery, and exile.

The last king of the ten tribes of Israel was wicked king Hoshea, who was a vassal of the king of Assyria. When Hoshea rebelled against Shalmaneser, king of Assyria, he was captured and imprisoned. Then after the fall of Samaria the entire Israelite population, apart from Judah and Benjamin, was deported to Assyria, never to return. There most of them eventually lost their tribal identities. All this happened because instead of repenting and turning to God, they became more and more degenerate. They actually despised and even murdered the prophets God sent to warn them; they rejected the Covenant God had made with their ancestors, and flouted all the loving warnings he had given them. In direct violation of God's commands they set up and worshipped calf idols, stars, Ashera, and Baal, and even offered their sons and daughters to these vile gods. Divination and sorcery, and other forbidden practices, were rife among the people, and in the end their wickedness exceeded the wickedness of the people God had determined to displace from the land of Canaan, in the first place. Through worshipping useless idols they themselves became subhuman and useless.

After centuries of holding back God eventually unleashed the curses of the Covenant, and rejected Israel as he had warned. The Assyrians had Samaria and the surrounding towns resettled with other conquered people. When lions invaded the towns and started killing off the new population, the king of Assyria concluded that the god of the land was angry. He had an Israelite priest brought back to teach the people how to worship God. Quite willing to add a new god to their bevy of gods, the new population attempted to put Jehovah on a par with their own gods. They then made priests from their own people instead of from Levites, and used the old worship sites and idols abandoned by the exiled Israelites. These practices were, of course, revolting to the one true God.

Meanwhile Hezekiah was king of Judah, and the best king the two remaining tribes ever had. He trusted God and remained faithful to God and his Covenant all his life. He rid the nation of idols, and everything connected with their worship. He even got rid of the bronze serpent that Moses had made, since the people had begun to burn incense to it. The Lord was with him in everything he did from rebelling and getting out from under the yoke of the king of Assyria, to defeating the surrounding Philistines.

However after several years of peace King Sennacherib of Assyria attacked and captured all the fortified cities of Judah. Instead of fighting back Hezekiah sent an apology to King Sennacherib, promising to pay whatever he demanded. He exacted such exorbitant taxes, that Hezekiah had to empty the royal coffers, the Temple coffers, and even had to strip the gold overlay from the doors and door posts of the Temple, to pay him.

In spite of this, King Sennacherib advanced on Jerusalem with proud taunts and blasphemy against God, and his ability to protect his people. King Hezekiah knew very well that Sennacherib and the Assyrian empire were sweeping all before them. He fasted and prayed and called on God to deliver Jerusalem. Isaiah the prophet was sent to give King Hezekiah a wonderful message of assurance of God's protection, and promise of a miraculous intervention. That night the angel of the Lord put to death a hundred and eighty-five thousand Assyrian soldiers, resulting in the withdrawal of King Sennacherib back to Nineveh. There while in a temple worshipping his idol god Nisrock, he was assassinated by two of his sons.

When Hezekiah, the best of kings, died many years later, he was succeeded by his son Manasseh, one of the worst of kings. Manasseh was notorious not only for his flagrant idol worship and its attendant devilish practices, but also for his callous slaughter of his own people, making Jerusalem's streets run with innocent blood.

Though God spoke to Manasseh and his people they paid no attention, with the result that God again used the Assyrians to bring his message home. Manasseh was taken prisoner, and with a hook in his nose and in bronze shackles, he was led away to Babylon. Only then did he cry out to God in repentance, and the Lord listened to him and took him back to Jerusalem and his kingdom. There he set in motion the abolition of idolatry and the reinstatement of the worship of the one true God, in a cleansed Temple. After Manasseh's fifty-five year reign, his wicked son Amon reigned for two years, until his assassination.

Judah, instead of taking warning from Israel's downfall, had followed her idolatrous example. In spite of warning after warning from the Lord through his prophets, in spite of battles lost and won, in spite of times of plenty and times of famine, Judah led by her kings also hurtled towards exile. Along the way there was one other good king, but the history of a king such as good King Josiah of Judah shows just how far downhill things had gone. The beautiful Temple Solomon had built, where God promised to dwell, lay in disrepair, and had been desecrated by an Asharah pole in the Temple, articles for the worship of the idol Baal, as well as quarters for male shrine prostitutes, and places where women did weaving for Asherah. Even the Book of the Law, which should have been copied for every new king, and read to the people every seven years, was lost. The Covenant was forgotten. In spite of Josiah's reforms and the dire warnings from Huldah, the prophetess, Judah returned to idolatry after Josiah's death under the rule of Jehoahaz his son, who reigned only three months before being carried away in chains to Egypt, by Pharoah Neco. His brother on becoming king was no better. He was of course, a vassal to King Nebuchadnezzar, king of Babylon, after the defeat of Egypt.

The taxes imposed by these foreign rulers were crippling, but as the remaining kings rebelled this brought on the fall of Jerusalem, exile for the people, the end of the kings of Judah, and the complete stripping and destruction of the Temple Solomon had built. It was burned and the walls of Jerusalem destroyed. Many of the inhabitants were killed while the remainder were marched off to Babylon to become slaves for seventy years as Jeremiah, the prophet, had predicted.

However because of his Covenant promises to the patriarchs, God did not destroy Israel completely, but preserved a remnant of Judah in captivity for his own purposes. They included the tribe of Benjamin, many Levites, and some Israelites who had been living near Jerusalem when it finally fell. In them the predictions of the prophets such as Isaiah, Jeremiah, and others would be fulfilled. I will leave you now."

With a quick bye Samuel left almost as quietly as he had come. Melvyn wandered some more through the lofty building with its disturbing displays of good kings and despots.

Chapter Nine

The Spirit explains

A voice behind Melvyn broke in:

"Kings like to throw their weight around and people in authority like to give themselves fancy titles. It's not going to be that way with you. Let the senior among you become like the junior; let the leader act the part of the servant."

Melvyn turned to see Immanuel. Melvyn's heart was strangely warmed and he was filled with an overwhelming desire to fall at this man's feet, and just stay there. Melvyn said nothing but Immanuel put his arm around Melvyn's shoulder and said, "I know, Melvyn. It's all right!"

"Do you know everything I think and feel?" Melvyn asked.

Immanuel said nothing but Melvyn heard a voice inside him say quite distinctly, "Don't be afraid, I've redeemed you. I've called your name. You're mine!"

"Strange how long forgotten Scripture seems to be invading my mind," Melvyn thought. Immanuel squeezed Melvyn's shoulder.

Melvyn paused briefly and looked again at the
portrait of handsome King David. "You were descended
from King David, Immanuel, were you not?" Melvyn
asked.

"Yes, everything prophesied about me in Scripture
was planned by me, the Father, and the Spirit, and it all
unfolded in my life on earth. Do you now see how our
plan for humanity began to take shape through the
centuries until your own time?"

"Not really! It all seems rather convoluted to me.
I can't see the point of much of it, and it all took such
a long time with so much misery along the way,"
Melvyn replied.

"Melvyn, it takes several generations to change the
framework through which cultures view themselves,
interpret the world, and their place in it. Many people
never think deeply about these things; they just accept
the assumptions of the people around them. Believing a
lie about God made Adam and Eve run away and hide
in the bushes, and things are seldom different today.
Believing lies about God has skewed the thinking of
humanity ever since, and their natural instinct is to run
as far as possible away from God. They become prisoners
of darkness and lies, although believing the truth about
God can set them free."

"Is that why you said you are the way, the truth, and
the life?" Melvyn asked.

"Indeed, but humanity finds it easier to go with the
flow, and believe the lie that God doesn't care about
them, or is powerless to prevent bad things happening
to them. The truth is that we love them to death. Indeed
we loved them and still love them through my death,
and on to resurrection life. I have showed you a little of

what resurrection life looks like, but due to your limited imagination, I can only give you a tiny taste of it. The reality is far beyond what anyone who is merely human can understand or imagine; it is too good to believe. It is better than your wildest, happiest dream."

"Immanuel, tell me the plan again. Help me to understand," Melvyn pleaded.

"The Holy Spirit is the best teacher. I will send her to you and she will help you recall and understand all I have been teaching you. She will help you make sense of it all," Immanuel promised. "Stay here and I will send my Spirit to you."

Melvyn sat in the palace gardens in the shade of a leafy vine. The Holy Spirit joined him and for some time sat quietly, saying nothing. Melvyn sat quietly too, awe pervading his mind as he waited for the Spirit to begin.

A voice like soft music over water came as balm to Melvyn's weary soul. He was enfolded by the mystery of a holy all-embracing love. He listened with amazement to the glorious revelation and the healing words, as if hearing good news for the first time in his life.

"Melvyn, we made the world out of a desire to share our love for each other with creatures that would be like us, able to love us and each other, able to reciprocate and communicate love. We made such a beautiful, good world with perfectly lovely creatures, and gave it all to humans to care for it, and look after it. Oh, what perfect loveliness there was on earth before the spoiling ...

Sadly, humans listened to the voice of a creature rather than the voice of God. Darkness invaded the human mind, and in no time humans began worshipping their fellow creatures, and even created things like the sun, moon, and stars. They did this when they could see us, and talk to us face to face. Now with darkened minds and hearts they cannot see us, or hear our voice speaking. Even when they turn to us they cannot sense us clearly; they must now trust and believe us, in spite of their muddle of mental confusion, and physical brokenness. I strive every day with humankind to make myself heard and understood, but with hardened hearts and depraved inclinations they keep rejecting my healing love. How do we reach you, how do we understand you, how do we win back our spoilt creation? Don't get me wrong, we foresaw the spoiling and prepared for each contingency in advance. It is just that the reality always seems worse than the foreseeing.

The Son, through whom all things were made and are held together, had to take on the fallen mind and the fallen flesh of humanity. Vicariously he had to live a life of unbroken oneness with God, in loving obedience to God knowing the cost. However the gift of a loving spotless life would be lost to humanity, if their dreadful disease of mind and body was not cured. As we foretold before the spoiling, death would be the consequence of alienation from God. There is no cure for sin and its corrupting consequences; it has to be destroyed by death. The one who had never sinned, or allowed the invasive darkness of the fallen human mind to penetrate his thinking, or the weakness of fallen human flesh to lead him astray, must give himself up to death as a substitute for those who really deserved to die.

Darkness and the corruption of the human mind and body could not be reverted, or patched up, and had to be destroyed to bring it to an end. To come through death to the resurrection of a new creation, humanity's death had to be in union with Christ, for since Christ had never sinned death had no hold over him. He gave himself to death taking humanity with him, and later he was raised by God from the dead, taking humanity to resurrected life in union with his new body."

"But I don't see that that can possibly be true. Things are just as bad now as they ever were," Melvyn interrupted.

"There are some things that humanity can only learn through experience. If we didn't allow you to get lost in your own darkness, and to suffer some of the consequences in your own darkened minds and bodies, you would never be convinced that we would go to any lengths to rescue you. We don't want robots or slaves. We want free humans who choose to love us and each other, who can live in harmony and joy in the new creation, after the final resurrection."

"That seems to make some sense, but I still don't see the whole picture," Melvyn conceded. "Do we really have to suffer murder, rape, injustice, genocide, war, famine, disease, just to learn to love you?"

"Let me take you through a short history of humankind from our point of view, just to help you see our plan more clearly. As I said before, we knew and prepared in advance for what people would do. But humanity did not know or believe how depraved they could become, if left to their own devices. We decided we had to let them see for themselves. Even today, after the world's long history of demonstrating the opposite, many people, and even many Christian, think that the world is improving. They imagine that through education, or some other program, they can do better and pull themselves up by their bootstraps, if only everyone would try harder.

Time after time people, including Israel the people we chose to bring the light of truth to the nations, persisted in going their own way. We had to give them up to their own will to let them see where it would all lead. Inevitably they ended up in such depravity and violence that, sick at heart, we had to step in again.

From the beginning, exiled by love from the Garden of Eden, but clothed with our compassionate grace, we continued to care for humanity. We kept communicating with those who had ears to hear us. You know the story of the next generation, how Cain murdered his brother Abel in spite of a stern forewarning from us. Have you any idea how many family members have murdered other family member since that day? Every day, that sin is repeated again and again, all over the world.

We let humanity get on with life but they stopped hearing us, or talking to us. Within a few generations of the spoiling, the world was filled with so much violence, that we were disgusted and decided to wipe out all humanity from the earth, apart from Noah and his family. We sent that generation to Hades until Christ visited them after his death with the good news of what he had done for them. Noah alone and his family, of all people alive at that time, lived in a right relationship with us, and with them we gave humanity a chance to start over afresh.

Within a very short time the world had once again slipped into corruption and pride, forgetting their Maker and their dependence on him for every breath they take. Their foolishness took the form of deciding to build the Tower of Babel for their own glory, which would only be a tower to the lies of their actual situation. We stopped them by the confusion of languages, but they still did not acknowledge the truth of our provision for their every need. In their foolishness they continued to believe lies, and thought that the gods of their own making were providing for them. We knew there was no cure for their wicked delusions unless we provided one, but they could not see this.

We had decided to teach humanity through one nation that would become a blessing to all the other nations. I'm talking, of course, of Abraham and the Children of Israel. We separated them from the other people of the earth, and through a Covenant relationship with them, tried to teach them bit by bit to understand how the Son would become a human to save humanity from sin and its consequences, and how they would fit into the picture. The Son of God would be the one who would be a mediator between divinity and humanity.

Abraham's own life was a series of experiences and revelations to help him understand God's plan. He was specially called and given promises that would change the world. He had to choose to believe God in spite of the circumstances and the trials of his life. His faith was tested many times. Promised that he would be the father of nations, he had to wait years for a legitimate son to be born to him. He was given circumcision as a sign of the Covenant, but in a strange experience of intense darkness it was revealed to him that his progeny would become slaves in Egypt, and it would be several centuries before they inherited the land promised to them.

In another test Abraham came to understand something of God the Father's heart, when he was called to sacrifice his beloved son Isaac. He was shown God's purpose, in the wonderful gift of a ram to be sacrificed at the last minute instead of Isaac. Isaac was not to be sacrificed but God's son would be sacrificed. Through these experiences and others he saw Christ's day, and rejoiced in God's provision of a perfect substitute sacrifice.

As prophesied in Abraham's vision, the Children of Israel became slaves in Egypt. They experienced the awful effects of the inhumanity of humans to each other. They experienced the helplessness of slaves under the brutal treatment of Pharaoh. They subsequently learned the meaning of Passover, redemption, the presence of God in a cloud and fire, and his loving care in the provision of water and daily bread for them, from heaven. Also we gave the Israelites the Torah, and the Covenant was renewed.

At the same time the tent of meeting with its animal sacrifices, its Holy of Holies containing the Ark of the Covenant with its mercy seat, was set up. Also the high priesthood, and the priesthood for tabernacle worship and instruction of the people, were all set in place. These were pictures of the heavenly realities and the future atoning work of the Son of God. In picture form, corruption, sin, death, mercy, forgiveness, healing, holy living, and communion with God in worship and blessing were displayed on a daily, monthly, and annual basis. This was to be God's on-going relationship with, and provision for his people until the time when symbol would become reality.

You have met Joshua and seen how eager the people were to thank and praise God for taking them to the Promised Land, and blessing them with peace and security. They were quite sure then they would always be faithful to God and the Covenant. You later met the judges, and realized how within a few generations the hearts and minds of most Israelites were seduced away, to embrace the idol gods of the peoples they had conquered. The pattern became backsliding and repentance, backsliding and repentance. The people who were to bring the light of truth, the hope of liberation and justice for the nations, in time became as corrupt as those they were supposed to enlighten. They brought God's reputation to disgrace among the heathen so that our name was blasphemed among the nations.

You know the history of the kings of Israel and Judah. We warned, we cajoled, we entreated them through the prophets, and through handing them over to heathen armies to kill, rape, plunder and pillage them. In this we showed ourselves patient, merciful, and above all faithful to the Covenant we had made with them. Under affliction they repented, and then when things settled down they once more slipped into their evil ways by oppressing the poor, forgetting our laws, trampling on the weak, and practicing all the abominations of pagan idol worship, and demon assisted black magic.

Our warnings through the prophets became more and more urgent as the dark cloud of annihilation and exile, promised curses of the Covenant, gathered over Israel and Judah. Instead of listening to the prophets, they mistreated and killed them, and every passing year the kings and people became more brutish and callous. Disaster overtook first Israel and then Judah. Invading Babylonian armies brutally slaughtered the people, the Temple was stripped and burned, and the walls of Jerusalem were pulled down. A pathetic remnant was herded off to Babylon to slavery and to disgrace.

There is a special programme going on at the moment. It is the interviewing of some of the prophets, at the time of the kings, who wrote, preached, and warned the kings and people of the consequences of their wicked ways. I think you would find it interesting and instructive. I'll take you there now.

When our people join us in our kingdom they are sometimes quite ignorant of their own history. Not all have had the privilege of having the Bible to read in their own language, or even the privilege of being able to read at all. On coming here their eyes are opened to many things, but all have much to learn. What better way than to meet the people who were pivotal characters in the drama of the everlasting Covenant? That way they begin to understand us more and more."

They walked through the garden and through the ornate opening of a large amphitheatre. People were sitting in rows on stone seats. The interviewer and the prophets were just taking their seats on a large, raised, semi-circular stage facing the audience, as Melvyn found a space and sat down. Everyone's attention was focused on the stage. Due to the amazing acoustics, the interviewer's voice and those of the others on stage could be heard through the whole amphitheatre.

Chapter Ten

The Prophets tell their Stories

"My name is Philippa, after my father, the evangelist. My three sisters, who like me were prophets during our previous life, are sitting beside our father. Beside them is the man you will know from Scripture as, 'the Ethiopian eunuch from the court of Queen Candace'. Eunuch no longer but still a great man of learning, it is good to see him and all of you here.

Throughout history many people have believed that God behaved differently under the Old Covenant from the New Covenant. Some have even claimed that God was cruel, vengeful, and bloodthirsty under the Old Covenant, and only with the coming of Christ did he become loving and kind. The prophets here will tell a different story – the story of our compassionate Creator, who has always loved us, and who never changes. They tell us the story of our God who has gone to unbelievable lengths to re-create us, and all creation, to be what he intended us to be from the beginning. He wants us, through union with Christ, to be included in the intimate circle of love that is God the Father, God the Son, and God the Holy Spirit.

The prophets will use the writings they composed during their previous lives on earth, to show that the character and purposes of God under the Old Covenant were always for the good of the whole world. The history of humanity moves forward from creation, to Fall, to Israel, to Christ's life, death, resurrection, ascension, and to the coming of the Holy Spirit, and the establishment of the church to bring the Gospel to all the nations. After that, comes the final resurrection of the dead, the judgement, and putting right of all wrongs, before the full establishment of Christ's everlasting kingdom on earth. Finally there will be the coming down of the New Jerusalem to earth, as heaven (God's dwelling place), and earth (our dwelling place), are joined together forever.

The election of Israel as a nation to bring the message that there was only one true God to the other nations, to be a 'light to the nations', you will recall was the purpose of their special relationship with God in the first place. God made this Covenant first with Abraham, and then renewed it with his descendants when he rescued them from Egypt and gave them the Law at Sinai. Through their experiences and through the Law, they would come to understand the plan of God to deal with the consequences of the Fall. A new vocabulary and new concepts had to be developed, rituals enacted in a special tabernacle and later a Temple, which would foreshadow the coming of Christ and his gathering up of everybody and everything in the spoilt creation, to bring them in union with his own body, to death. The decay of the cosmos could only be halted by death, and reversed in recreation. The Messiah had to die to bring sin and its consequences to an end. He could then bring it to a completely new life in his own resurrection.

There are four areas we are going to examine in this discussion:

1) The specific evils that brought the Covenant people to exile.
2) The patience and efforts of God to avert the exile.
3) The plan of God to end the exile and so keep his Covenant with Abraham and his children.
4) The Messiah and his kingdom as foretold by the prophets.

Isaiah, we know your book covered all of these four areas, and so if you give us your perspective, the others can then add their further insights to the discussion."

"Thank-you, Philippa. Let me begin then with the evils that the Israelites were perpetrating that totally broke their commitment to the Covenant, and really grieved the Lord, when I lived on earth.

The Israelites were the ones who were supposed to show the world that there was only one real God, and that he created the world. They were the ones that should have been showing the world the foolishness of worshipping gods that were only bits of wood, silver, and gold. The nations around not only made idols but were worshipping elements of creation such as the sun, the moon, and the stars, instead of the Creator. Unlike all the other ancient religions, Judaism never confused the created with the Creator.

In my day while the Israelites were still sacrificing and observing the feasts God had appointed, honouring him with their lips, their hearts were far from him. They had dared to set up idols alongside the worship of God, as if they were on a par with the one true God. They further angered God by assimilating in idol and nature worship, the vile practices of these demon gods from the surrounding nations. These included shrine prostitution, passing their children through fire to dedicate them to demons, consulting the spirits of the dead, using mediums and magic, all of which God detested and which he had forbidden in the Law.

The prophets, false ones of course, not only approved of such behaviour but lied to the people by telling them that as long as they kept sacrificing to God, he would not mind them worshipping other gods. They further misled the people by teaching them the finer points of the vile practices associated with the worship of idols. As always happens, when people follow vile practices their behaviour becomes increasingly degenerate and inhuman. The princes began oppressing the people and stealing land and houses, even from orphans and widows. Unjust laws that promoted greed and bloodshed were enacted. Corruption was rife, with judges and other officials taking bribes. Good was called evil and evil good.

Not only the rich powerful men, but their wives too became arrogant and evil. They thought only of flirting, decking themselves out in expensive anklets, bangles, earrings, nose rings, signet rings, charm bracelets, necklaces, headbands, veils, fine robes, capes, cloaks, purses, using fine perfumes and walking with mincing steps to attract attention to themselves. With their husbands, the rulers and elders, they crushed the weak and ground down the faces of the poor to provide grist for their vanity.

Could God turn a blind eye to such horrible wickedness and oppression? He could not. Did God want to bring the curses of the Covenant on his elect people? He did not. Through me he called out to the people to return to him, to throw out their idols and their vile rituals, to seek justice for the oppressed, the fatherless and the widows, and to acknowledge that there was only one living God. He poured out loving words and promises of blessing, patiently trying to cajole them back to sanity and integrity. He did not want to send them into exile but if they continued in their wickedness he would have no choice but to be faithful to the Covenant, and apply its curses for disobedience. He would not allow injustice and greed to go unpunished, and the poor to be ruthlessly exploited. He would not allow his name to be associated with idols. He warned them that a cruel and ruthless nation would invade the land, stripping them of their beautiful homes, their crops and belongings, their wives and children, and dragging those not slaughtered into slavery and exile.

Though they persisted in being faithless to the Covenant, God promised he would not forget his Covenant with them. Even in exile, when they realised their folly and turned back to him, he would be gracious and take them back to their homeland and bless them. Then he would restore justice to the land and her people, with judges, rulers, teachers of the Law, and priests who would honour God, and bring peace and security to the land again. Though his people would suffer seventy years of humiliation and cruel exile, he would bring them back to their own land, when they acknowledged their wickedness and folly.

He warned he would use the Assyrians as a tool to inflict the curses of the Covenant on his people, but he would also punish the King of Assyria for going too far. Instead of just defeating Judah and seizing loot and plunder, the invader would try to annihilate God's people. God had made a Covenant promise to his people that he would send a saviour who would set up an everlasting kingdom of love, peace, and justice. He would not allow the complete destruction of his people, as this would break his Covenant promises, and thwart his good plans for his new creation."

"Thank-you, Isaiah. Could you fill out a little for us the picture you were given of this saviour, and the new kingdom he would set up?" Philippa asked.

"Certainly, although at the time, my understanding of the coming of the Messiah, and how his kingdom would be established, was quite vague and sketchy. With hindsight I can see the meaning of what I wrote much more clearly. This king was to be born of a virgin, the Spirit of the Lord would rest on him, and he would be elect of God to bring justice to the nations, in gentleness and meekness, not in showy warfare and cruelty. He himself would be the embodiment of God's Covenant faithfulness, and a light to the Gentiles, bringing healing and renewal to the whole world.

He would be the son of David whose kingdom would know no end, and yet he would be rejected and despised by those he came to save. He would be a suffering saviour whose life on earth would be one of sorrow, grief, and eventual undeserved, unjust death. By taking on himself the sin and disease of the whole world, he opened up a way for us to be healed and recreated in him. He would be the true sin offering depicted in the sacrificial rituals of the Jerusalem Temple. He would be upheld by his anger at everything that was destroying his good creation. Blood splattered and alone he would fight evil by dying, and not by the use of the sword.

His grave, provided by a wealthy man, would not be the end of him and he would go on to see resurrection life for himself, and the nations he came to save. Who can sum up the kindness, the compassion, and utterly extravagant love of our God and Saviour? To him belongs homage and glory forever and ever!"

"Yes, yes! Forever and forever we will praise and love and adore him," came a spontaneous chorus from the audience.

"We now know that all this was fulfilled in Immanuel's life, death, resurrection, and ascension."

"Yes indeed, Isaiah! Thank you! Maybe you would add your experience to that, Jeremiah?" Philippa suggested.

"Yes, Philippa," Jeremiah answered. "My experience in many ways mirrored Isaiah's. Although my ministry began under good king Josiah, who influenced Judah for good, many of the people still persisted in turning to idols and the practices of the nations around them. Injustice and greed were rife, and I was sent to warn them to turn from their wicked ways so that exile, the curse of the Covenant, would not overtake them. Sadly after Josiah died, things really went from bad to worse.

They did not listen to me or consider the loving kindness and patience of God. Their own prophets told them that they were doing just fine, and that God would bless them with continued peace and prosperity. Still my message disturbed them and they hated me. I was continually threatened with death. I was beaten, lowered into a deep muddy pit, spent years in prison, and only with help from the few believers left, did I escape.

God often used parables to teach me and the people what he was really like. One time I was sent to a potter to watch him at his trade. The pot he was making was marred in his hands but he scooped it up, reworked the clay, and produced a fine pot. God promised he would do this with the people of Jerusalem but they wanted none of it.

Another time I was sent by God to buy a clay jar from the potter. I then had to take some of the elders and priests to the Potsherd Gate. There I was told to preach the word of God, and I was told to condemn the idolatry, the shedding of innocent blood, the sacrificing of the children to idols, and the other evil practices that were going on in the city. Afterwards I had to break the pot before them, to show them that once the fire-hardened pot was broken it could no longer be repaired, unlike the spoiled clay pot that could still be reshaped.

After that I had to go to the Temple, and preach to all the stubborn people there that God was going to bring disaster on them, because they persisted in ignoring his warnings. I was beaten and put in the stocks for my trouble but I could not suppress the words of the Lord. I had to keep on prophesying, setting before them the way of life and the way of death. It was like a fire in my belly that I could not quench. I wept buckets for my people but they were impossible.

Eventually when Jerusalem was surrounded by the Babylonians in a two year siege, the king at the time,

Zedekiah, sent for me and asked what he should do. He was a vassal king who had rebelled. The former king of Judah was already in Babylon, in exile. I told Zedekiah he must surrender to the Babylonians, if his life and that of his family were to be spared, but he procrastinated and did not do what God asked him to do. Sadly he was taken captive, his sons and nobles were killed in his sight, and then his own eyes were put out. He was taken to Babylon in bronze shackles, and there he eventually died in prison. His palace was burned, as were all the fine houses of the rich. I was put in chains with the other prisoners but Nebuchadnezzar, king of Babylon, had given orders that I should be well treated and I was released.

I was then put under the protection of Gedaliah, who had been appointed governor over the very small remnant of poor people left in the land. When Gedaliah was later assassinated, the people were thrown into great turmoil fearing the Babylonians would come and slaughter them, or carry them off into exile. Most thought they should flee to Egypt. They turned to me and begged me to ask God what they should do, swearing to obey the answer whether good or bad. I willingly agreed, and God told me to tell them to stay where they were and he would protect them. If they disobeyed, they would be killed or die in Egypt.

The leaders of the group then accused me of lying and wanting to betray them to the Babylonians. In spite of their vow to the Lord they forced everyone, including me, away to Egypt. God then warned me the Babylonians would attack Egypt and defeat it. Again I warned them of this but they would not listen. When further evils things occurred, they decided the reason disaster had befallen them was because they had stopped worshipping the Queen of Heaven. They resumed sacrificing to this false goddess, believing she had brought them prosperity in the old days. I warned them that not only would Egypt be defeated, but the temples of the idol gods of the Egyptians would be burned. These things happened as the Lord had forewarned, and very few of our people ever returned to Judah again.

In spite of all this, God promised that he would make a new Covenant with his people, writing his Law on their hearts. He also promised that he would send a Branch of David – we now know the Messiah – who would rule wisely and do what was right and just in the land."

"Thanks, Jeremiah. You were a faithful and compassionate servant of God, and you suffered for your faithfulness. Ezekiel, maybe you would now tell us your story?"

"My pleasure, Philippa," Ezekiel answered. "My ministry began as a priest. After Jerusalem had been defeated, I, King Jehoichin, and others were taken into exile. There God called me to be a prophet to warn those left in Jerusalem that if they did not repent of their wickedness, Jerusalem would be sacked, and the Temple stripped and burned. Zedekiah had been made vassal king by the Babylonians, but he was no better than his predecessor. He did not listen to Jeremiah and he did not listen to me. As Jeremiah has told you, he rebelled against the Babylonians and Jerusalem was sacked, the Temple was stripped of its sacred treasures and burned to the ground. Zedekiah died sightless and childless in prison in Babylon. During his reign I warned the people of the fate that was to befall the Temple.

God also showed me visions of the disturbing idolatry, and defilement of the Temple, that was taking place in Jerusalem, even at the hands of the priests and Levites, who at the same time kept on performing the Temple rituals, as prescribed in the Law. Through a hole in the wall of the Temple I saw horrible insects and animals portrayed on the walls, and elders and priests offering incense at their personal shrines to idol gods. God was sickened, but he was still loath to give up on them.

I had many difficult living parables to enact to show the people what would befall them if they persisted in their wickedness. Once I had to make a drawing of Jerusalem on a clay tablet with siege works, ramps, camps, and battering rams around it, and I had to lie on my left side behind an iron pan facing it for three hundred and ninety days, the same number as the years that Israel had been unfaithful to God. I had to do the same on my right side for forty days as a sign to Judah of the years of her unfaithfulness to God. I had to be tied down with ropes to keep me from turning from one side to the other during this time. Before I lay down I had to prepare food and put it in a storage jar to eat during this ordeal, as well as a ration of water. This depicted the rationing of food and water that the people of Jerusalem would have to suffer, during the upcoming siege of Jerusalem.

Another time I had to cut off my hair and beard and divide the hair into portions that were burned, cut up with a sword, and thrown to the wind. A very few strands were reserved and tucked into the folds of my clothes but even some of them I had to burn in fire, as fire would destroy Jerusalem. I had to preach against the continued wickedness of princes, priests, and people, even although it was all to no avail.

Hardest of all I had to suffer the death of my beloved wife without mourning (I was only allowed to groan quietly at her loss), to portray the suffering of the Jews when their beloved Temple would be destroyed, and they were slaughtered or dragged off to exile.

During this time I was given many visions of Heaven, God's dwelling place, and of future events which would occur before and after Messiah came. Often I was afraid and faint from these visions as they were unbearably real, and frighteningly glorious.

God showed me that though the people were faithless to him and the Covenant, he would never be faithless to them. After the Temple was destroyed, as I had prophesied, words of hope and consolation came to me for the people in exile. They were to settle down in exile and plant crops, marry, have children and build homes for themselves, as exile would continue for many years to come. God would not forget them, and their children would return to their land. God would be their God and they would be his people, never again to look to idols for help. The countries who hated them would be punished, until they came to realize who the one and only true God is. They too would then be blessed. A new Temple would be built where God's glory would dwell, and all the faithful would be blessed. Part of this came true at the appointed time and part is taking place now, in the Kingdom of our God and Prince Immanuel. The name of the city became God-Is-There."

"I know there is a lot more you could tell us, Ezekiel, but we can all read your book or ask you, if we want to learn more. For our present purpose the important thing is the gist of what you are saying, which is that God is love and he never was anything else. He showed himself true to all his Covenant promises, and he brought about the good plans he had to recreate the cosmos. It is helpful to get some of the background to your book before we read it again. That way it comes to life more, because we understand where you are coming from."

"I am always available to expand on anything that seems obscure."

"Thank you! I'm sure some of us will want to take advantage of the offer, and I am sure the other prophets are open to giving the same help."

They all nodded, and then Philippa turned to Hosea.

"Hosea, we would normally hear from Daniel at this point but his story is so well know and so dramatic, that a live show, complete with lions and a fiery furnace for his three friends is being staged later on. Daniel's visions of the rise and fall of the empires of Babylon, Persia, Egypt, Greece and Rome with their pagan kings and tyrants will also be featured, as will his visions of Messiah's kingdom and times.

Right now we would like to hear from you. Unlike the prophets we have heard from so far, you prophesied in Samaria, and to the Northern kingdom that broke away from Solomon's son and the Davidic kings."

"That's right, Philippa, but the behaviour of the people was much the same in the north and south. Instead of being grateful to God for plentiful harvests and other blessings, the people started sacrificing their food to idols. My family life became a living parable of God's love for his faithless, idolatrous people. I had to marry a prostitute, and I had to love her and provide generously for her. She, like faithless Israel, used what I provided for her to buy herself lovers and leave me. God said I was to buy her back, forgive her, love her and show her kindness. Israel, like my adulterous wife, was promised blessings and love.

God was so patient and loving to us. He did not break Covenant with us though we broke Covenant with him, and refused his love, scornful of his pleas."

"Your story is a powerful one, Hosea. How loving our God is. Thank you, Hosea. Joel, your story is of a different time, a time when a plentiful harvest was destroyed by a huge plague of locusts."

"Yes, God tried everything to bring us back to himself. Kindness and prosperity did not entice us to keep Covenant with God, and so he gave us plague and famine to see if that would bring us to our senses. As you can guess it did not, and yet even in our misery, God promised us a new beginning. A day of renewal was coming, when God would pour out his Spirit on everyone. As the Book of Acts relates, my prophesy was fulfilled on the day of Pentecost and things have never been the same since. Let me repeat those glorious words:

'I will pour out my Spirit
on every kind of people:
Your sons will prophesy,
also your daughters;
Your young men will see visions,
your old men dream dreams.
When the time comes,
I'll pour out my Spirit
On those who serve me, men and women both,
and they'll prophesy.'

God was certainly loving and kind to us, and in spite of our wickedness in breaking Covenant with him he remained faithful to us, and fulfilled all his promises to us."

"Indeed he did. Thank you, Joel. I saw that prophesy come true in my own life and that of my sisters. Now we turn to Amos. Amos, your ministry took place in the Northern Kingdom at a time when Israel was very prosperous financially, but you yourself were from the Kingdom of Judah. You were a shepherd and you also tended sycamore-fig trees, yet God sent you to prophesy to Israel."

"That's true, Philippa. The nation of Israel was prosperous but their gains were for the most part ill-gotten, and the poor were exploited. Many people lived in beautiful stone houses with sumptuous ivory inlaid furniture, and they dined on the best of food, while being entertained by talented musicians. Yet God saw the terrible wickedness that underpinned the life styles of the rich, for corruption and bribery were rife, and justice was denied to the weak. In addition Nazirites, who pledged to never drink wine, were forced to do so, and prophets were ordered not to prophesy. The Covenant was forsaken and idol worship, and its attendant immorality, proliferated. God compared his people unfavourably to the wicked heathen nations he had thrown out of the land to make way for Israel in the first place. He warned them that they would suffer the same punishment as these heathen nations he had destroyed, if they did not repent and start keeping the Covenant.

Above all God was sickened by their hypocritical worship of him and proclaimed:

'I can't stand your religious meetings.
    I'm fed up with your conferences and conventions.
I want nothing to do with your religious projects,
    your pretentious slogans and goals.
I'm sick of your fund-raising schemes,
    your public relations and image making.
I've had all I can take of your noisy ego-music.
    When was the last time you sang to *me*?
Do you know what I want?
    I want justice – oceans of it.
I want fairness – rivers of it.
    That's what I want. That's *all* I want.'

He vowed, 'I'll send a famine through the whole country.
    It won't be food or water that's lacking, but my Word'
    As always, though God would have to punish their wickedness and avenge the wronged, he would not forget his part in the Covenant, and the promises he had made to set up an everlasting kingdom, where justice and love would prevail."

"How wonderful and kind our God is. Thank you, Amos. Do you have anything to add to the picture the other prophets have painted for us?" Philippa asked turning to Michah, when Amos had finished.

"Well, I was sent to warn both Jerusalem and Samaria of the judgement that must come upon them if they continued in their idolatry, and their oppression of the poor and weak. The whole underlying system of government and commerce was corrupt, as it was in the days of the other prophets. God could not continue to claim he was a just and loving God while continuing to let corruption, and cruelty, flourish unchecked. His beloved people had to be disciplined to bring them to their senses. As with the other prophets, God promised me that a Saviour would come, one from Bethlehem in Judah, who would rule in justice and bring peace to the whole earth," Michah explained. "We now know who that is."

Habakkuk then added, "Yes, but what I could not understand at the time was why God was letting the wicked flourish, while the righteous were being downtrodden and robbed of their homes, fields, and inheritances. There was no justice left in the land. His answer filled me with consternation because he spelled out that the Babylonians, that cruel nation, would be used to devastate the whole land. He did however promise me that a day was coming when, 'the earth would be filled up with awareness of GOD's glory as the waters cover the sea'."

"How wonderful! God does keep his promises," Philippa smiled. "Zephaniah, I believe God's message through you was the same?"

"Yes, the Lord promised that after dealing with his people in judgement, he would destroy all the heathen gods, and all the nations would worship him in their own lands."

"Israel was to be a light to the nations. God loves all his creation and even before Messiah's reign was inaugurated, God often reached out to heathen nations in love. Obediah, I believe you were sent to warn the descendants of Esau to repent of their wicked ways, especially the way they ignored the plight of their kinsmen in Jerusalem when it was overcome by alien armies. And you, Jonah, were actually angry with God for loving the people of Nineveh, and forgiving their sin?" Philippa continued looking in the direction of both men. They smiled and nodded.

"I'm afraid God had some tough lessons to teach me in that regard," Jonah admitted. "I had to learn that you can't run from God. He is the God of the whole world. He made everyone and loves everyone. I must be the only prophet who did not want my listeners to repent. I complained to God when Nineveh repented, 'God! I knew it – when I was back home, I knew this was going to happen! That's why I ran off to Tarshish! I knew you were sheer grace and mercy, not easily angered, rich in love, and ready at the drop of a hat to turn your plans of punishment into a program of forgiveness!

So, God, if you won't kill them, kill me! I'm better off dead!'

Can you believe it? I really thought I had the right to be angry, until the Lord showed me how absolutely selfish I was, and how unlike my God. I had a lot to learn."

"I guess we all did, Jonah. We had to learn that Israel was elected for a purpose, and not just for herself. Nahum, you did not get the same response when you were given a prophecy against Nineveh?" Philippa asked.

"No, by my time, Nineveh was in a sad state and ripe for God's judgement. They were a very cruel people, sadistic in fact. When their end came many nations heaved a sigh of relief and celebrated their downfall with great joy."

"The eventual return of the Jews from exile in Babylon is another story for another time. Our purpose today was to examine the love, patience, and long-suffering of our God in dealing with the unfaithfulness of his chosen people. He has not changed for he always was and always is and always will be love," Philippa concluded.

Chapter Eleven

On the Shores of a Great Lake

At this point the Spirit caught Melvyn up in her strong arms and carried him away to the shores of a great lake. There Immanuel was cooking food on a charcoal fire. A large buff coloured akita dog bounded up and nuzzled her head under Melvyn's hand. Some cats and other animals were sunning themselves on the rocks. Children were playing in the water and in the sand. Several adults were swimming, or sitting in small groups discussing things. A serene angel handed Melvyn a plate of food from Immanuel's fire. Melvyn sat on a rock savouring the food, observing his surroundings and soaking in the atmosphere. He was intensely aware of the absolute vitality, health, and joy of the people and animals around him. Indeed the very rocks and water seemed to be breathing out contentment. As he ate he stopped analysing, and let the peace and glory invade his being.

When he finished eating, he looked around again. The distant mountains offset the meadows in his midrange view. Wild flowers were growing profusely in the crevices of the rocks where he was sitting. At his feet water lapped on the sand. It all seemed familiar enough, and yet somehow more alive than any reality he had ever known before.

The swish of powerful wings, and the chuckling of babies, made Melvyn look up. To his astonishment, a huge angel was flying low with several babies on his back all holding on to his hair, and a young boy in his arms.

Immanuel had called a man and a woman to his side. The angel had landed at Immanuel's feet and the little ones scrambled to the couple.

"Mamma, daddy," they lisped to the astonished couple.

The boy pushed to the front. "Remember me?" he asked with glee.

"Findley!" the couple cried, rising to their feet and engulfing the boy with hugs and kisses. "You're alive?"

"Of course, I've always been alive. Immanuel took me when I was so sick and made me all better, and kept me with him, and now you've come as he said you would," Findley beamed.

Joy beyond description invaded the parents as they hugged, and wept, and laughed at the sight of their boy.

Immanuel gently interrupted, "Meet your other children! These are the children of your union too. They never survived even to childhood, but I kept them safe and loved and cared for, in my kingdom."

The couple, babies crawling all over them, were so bewildered with absolute delight they could hardly speak. They clung to Immanuel and laughed and laughed.

"Are all these babies your brothers and sisters, Findley?"

"Yes, we have such fun. Aren't they wonderful? Come and see all our friends!"

Findley escorted the gurgling babies and the dazed couple to the waiting angel who led them all away.

Melvyn remembered being told that his own mother had had a miscarriage before he was born. Perhaps he had a sibling in this wonderful country. He was trying to take everything in. He must have dozed off during his reverie. The next thing Melvyn was conscious of was Immanuel taking his hand, and leading him through the narrow streets of an ancient city. They stopped by the open door of a thick walled house. Inside a group of men were furtively discussing something with each other.

"I saw it with my own eyes. The man was blind. I had often seen him before, begging outside the Temple gate. He touched his eyes and the man could see. We know that's one of the things Messiah is going to do – open the eyes of the blind."

"I was on the road when he healed ten lepers and one of them was a Samaritan. Wouldn't you know it – the Samaritan was the only one who ran back and said, 'Thanks!'"

"I've heard he brought a dead girl back to life, and a young man they were carrying out to be buried."

"All the signs are there: healing the sick, casting out demons, raising the dead, and feeding five thousand people with five loaves and two fishes."

"Yes, we all saw that, but still he doesn't seem to be much of a warrior, or to have much of the Elijah spirit in him. Elijah called down fire from heaven to destroy

God's enemies. How is he going to get rid of the Romans for us and set up the Kingdom of Heaven? Talk's not going to do it."

"No, and he does say the strangest things. I heard him say if a soldier forces you to carry his tack for one mile you should carry it two miles for him. Now what kind of advice is that?"

"That seems pretty lame to me. Now if he had said, when you hand him back his tack, be sure and knife him through the ribs when he's picking up his bags, that would be Messiah talk."

"Still John the Baptist certainly seemed to think he was the Messiah."

"Yes, and look what happened to him. Surely if this fellow is the Messiah, he would have got John out of prison and deposed that traitor Herod. Herod's no king – just a puppet of Rome, lining his own purses and sleeping with his brother's wife."

"Keep your voice down. That kind of talk will get all our heads off."

"It's been such a long time of waiting for the promises to be fulfilled. Sure we are back in our land and the Temple is almost rebuilt, but we're still under the rule of foreigners. We are still in exile ..."

"Yes! It's a far cry from Zion being the centre of the earth, and the nations bringing tribute to us."

"Our ancestors did sin terribly. We brought the exile on ourselves."

"John said the kingdom was at hand."

"This fellow, Jesus, is saying it is here. The Pharisees say if we keep Torah the kingdom will come. At the same time most of them are raring for a revolution. As for the Sadducees, priests, and scribes, they seem to be more concerned with leading a quiet life, than being bothered about the promised kingdom."

"Yes, as long as they are comfortable they don't care much what happens to us. They just keep in with the Romans. Of course John wasn't too happy with the Pharisees and Sadducees either. He didn't like the way they looked down on us common folks, or the way they take such pride in Abraham being their father, as if he wasn't ours."

"Jesus has had several clashes with them too. They are always trying to trip him up, but he is too clever by half for them. He always has his answer ready. It almost seems as if he can read their minds, and he is always a step ahead of them. He pours scorn on their piety which confiscates widows' houses to pay the Temple taxes, leaving them and their children destitute."

"Quite right too, as if that was any kind of mercy or justice."

"Something has got to happen soon. Life just seems to be getting harder and harder for all of us. The tax collectors are getting greedier and greedier by the day. We all keep talking revolt, but the few who have tried it end up crucified. Talk is not going to get us anywhere. Why doesn't this fellow Jesus use his powers to flatten the Romans? We need force not words."

"I've heard him warning that if we don't repent and live the kingdom, another exile worse than any before will strike us."

The light seemed to fade and then Melvyn found himself among crowds of excited people lining the street. They were cutting down branches and throwing them and their cloaks, on the road. They were shouting at the top of their voices, "Hosanna to the Son of David!"

A man on a donkey appeared flanked by twelve attendants. Everybody was excited. Melvyn heard snatches of conversations, as the people talked to each other:

"This is the Messiah!"

"Jesus is riding into Jerusalem at last! He's going to free the city and take the throne!"

"We're going to be rid of the Romans at last!"

"Everything will be different. It's as the prophets have said – the nations will bring us taxes instead of us paying taxes to foreigners. We are God's special people and he is fighting for us!"

"Hosanna to David's Son!" the children shouted.

So the talk and shouts and celebrations went on. Melvyn watched them enter the city and the Temple precincts. The religious leaders gathered around and frowned. They were not happy to hear what the children were chanting and tried to get Jesus to stop them, but he just quoted the saying, "From the mouths of children and babies I'll furnish a place of praise."

Melvyn knew the end of the story. Immanuel was crowned with thorns and nailed to a Roman cross and left to die. Above him an inscription spelled out his crime in Aramaic, Greek, and Latin: "THIS IS JESUS, THE KING OF THE JEWS".

Melvyn again sensed Immanuel beside him. Looking up he asked, "Why didn't you destroy the Romans and set up your kingdom by force there and then? The people were all ready to worship you. You had the power."

"You mean I should have fought darkness with darkness? I should have become the king of an unhealed people still rife with sin and injustice, diseased in mind and body, in a world blighted by disasters of every kind? The Devil offered me that kind of throne three years before, in exchange for worshipping him."

"You could have changed all that with one command."

"Yes, Melvyn! You suggested much the same solution when we discussed the exile of Adam and Eve, from the Garden of Eden. I thought I explained then that we wanted real people, not puppet people, or robots. We love with real love, and we want our human image bearers to love with real love. We want a whole renewed world with whole renewed people, where love and justice reign. We want a people healed in mind and body from the inside out."

"I'm sorry! Yes, you did tell me. You told me that only by the death of sinful humanity, joined to your humanity, could sin and death be destroyed. Only in union with you could humanity be brought through death to resurrection, and the cosmos be recreated whole and healed again. Of course, I see now that the kind of kingdom you would have had by defeating the Romans, and setting up your power base in Jerusalem, would be nothing like the beautiful renewed earth with its amazing people, you showed me before. They are full of love and life just like you, Immanuel. A powerful kingdom of broken people, on a sick earth, would not suit you at all."

"Now you see at last," Jesus replied. "Darkness had to be fought with light and hate with love. The Evil One blinded the nations and blinded Israel. He found no foothold in me. As the true Son of God, Son of Man, Son of Abraham and Son of David, I became 'the true to

God Israelite' who carried away the sin of the world, and set up the Kingdom of God on earth. I was the true scapegoat, as well as the sacrificed goat, that ended all picture sacrifices. The battle is won. Re-creation has begun. The good news is being preached all over the world, to those who have ears to hear and eyes to see. My Spirit, my messengers, and my people proclaim the Gospel in all kinds of ways every day. The Kingdom of God is spreading in the world, like yeast in a batch of dough."

"I think I see the plan a lot clearer now," Melvyn conceded. "But why did you let the Romans destroy the Temple Herod had rebuilt? It was such a beautiful building by all reports, and why let all those Jews perish in AD70?"

"Destroy this Temple and in three days I will rebuild it. The destruction of the earthly building was symbolic. It was a small loss. Beautiful buildings will abound in my new earth, more beautiful than the most beautiful buildings ever seen on earth before. The Temple now is a living Temple made up of all my people. I live among them, and they join me continually in worship. About the unbelieving Jews – I had warned them time after time what would happen to them if they rejected me, and rebelled against the Romans. I told everyone who would listen that they must flee from Jerusalem when they saw the armies surrounding it, and escape to the hills at once. I told them the Temple would be utterly destroyed, and also the people left in the city. Those who listened escaped, while those who did not listen suffered horrendous barbarism. The believers did listen and leave. They did not suffer the horrors of those left behind in Jerusalem.

For many years after my death and resurrection, the Gospel was preached to everyone in Jerusalem, as well as to the whole world. We waited many years before giving up. Every opportunity was extended to the Jewish people to believe, but as in the days of Noah only a very few believed. Those who did believe were often persecuted and thrown out of the synagogues, by their fellow citizens.

You will remember that when I died the curtain to the Holy of Holies was torn in two from the top to the bottom. Instead of realizing that the Temple symbols had now been fulfilled in reality, when I the true high priest took my own blood, into the true Holy of Holies in heaven, the priests rushed to repair the old curtain. They did not realize the pictorial purpose of the old curtain, and that the old sacrifices were now fulfilled, and so were obsolete and no longer needed. They refused to listen to the truth. They imagined they were doing God a service by killing those who were preaching that I am the Son of God, and the Lamb of God that took away the sin of the world. They refused to believe that those who believe in me are now the new Temple where we dwell – I in them, and they in me. They did not believe I had been resurrected.

I saw the continuing unbelief of the people when I lived in Israel before I ascended to the Father, and it made me weep over Jerusalem, yearning for them to come to me to become whole. I could see that in their rejection of me they would fight with the tools of darkness against the Romans, and get crushed for their pains. The Temple was never rebuilt because my people are my Temple, and the sacrificial system was never restored, because my sacrifice was the one true sacrifice that ended all other atonement sacrifices. The blood of bulls, sheep, and goats could never take away sin, but only pointed to the one sacrifice that counted, the once for all sacrifice of the Son of God."

"Did that change the constitution of the people who could now call themselves Children of Abraham – didn't the Apostle Paul say something about that? Didn't he say that the Children of Abraham, the true Jews, are not those who are only Jews outwardly or ethnically, but all Jews and Gentiles together who believe in you?"

"Exactly! We promised Abraham, through an everlasting Covenant, that all the nations of the earth would be blessed through him, and his children would be as numerous as the sand on the seashores. We did not change the Covenant. I fulfilled the Covenant conditions for Israel and the world, and in me all the nations of the earth are blessed. Thus believers, Jews plus Gentiles who believe in me, are the true children of Abraham."

"Though I am beginning to see the big picture from your point of view, I must say that I don't see much evidence of the work of your kingdom taking place on earth where I live. Things seem to be going along much as they ever did – wars and rumours of war and disasters every other day," Melvyn remarked.

"I'll show you," Immanuel promised. "I'm sure it doesn't look like anything you imagined – my work never does! I was not the kind of Messiah the Jews imagined would solve their problems and set the world to rights; so why should things be any different in the unbeliever's eyes in your day?

Come and let me show you how and where the kingdom is advancing!"

Chapter Twelve

The Advance of the Kingdom

Melvyn and Immanuel approached a fisherman's cottage on the outskirts of a small island town. A woman with soil-stained hands was smiling at her husband, as they heaved heavy sacks of potatoes into a shed, and covered them with straw.

"That's the last of the main crop in for the winter, Mary. We've had a fine crop this year. God is good to us," the husband smiled back.

"Yes indeed, Hamish. I think I'll get one of the girls to take a sack to the two old sisters up the road. Then there's poor Jean down the road, bringing up her large family, all on her own. She's so crippled with arthritis she's finding it more and more difficult to keep up with the housework. I have a carpet sweeper I don't need, and I think I should give it to her."

"Mary, you do what you can to help them. The least we can do is to share the bounty we've been given."

A little later a young girl emerged from the house carrying a half sack of potatoes. She went in the direction of an old house, set apart from the fishermen's cottages on a nearby hill. Two other daughters emerged headed in the opposite direction, one with a similar bag of potatoes and the other carrying a carpet sweeper.

"This is my kingdom in action. My people look out for those in need, and with generous hearts give them whatever they can, to alleviate suffering. It gladdens my heart to see them doing this for me," Immanuel said turning to Melvyn.

"For you?" Melvyn quizzed.

"Yes, if they are doing it for even for the least significant of my people, they are doing it for me."

"But it's only potatoes! You have plenty of these in your kingdom fields. What's the big deal?" Melvyn remonstrated.

"They are sharing what they have, even although they have only modest means, and a large family of their own to feed. They are thinking of others, and their generous hearts are being prepared for life in my kingdom, in the age to come. There all inequities will be righted, and the earth will again produce abundantly with no thorns and thistles. Nobody will suffer a lack of anything good, and every heart will yearn to serve others and bring them joy."

Whisked away to a large city Melvyn saw an open door in a small semi-detached row house. A kindly middle-aged woman was welcoming a pair of shy foreign students into her home. Her husband, and two of their children who bore a close resemblance to their father, carried luggage from their car, into the house.

Inside the smell of dinner cooking wafted out to greet the guests. A large table was set for twelve. A young mother, another daughter of the generous couple, was attempting to wash the hands of several of her small children, but they were a lot more interested in sizing up the newcomers. Everyone welcomed the students and then sat down to eat.

One of the foreign students explained in broken English the predicament he and his fellow student had encountered, over mixed up accommodation arrangements, and how Katy and Russ, students themselves, had found them stranded in the city centre. They had called their parents for emergency help.

"That couple keep their home open to strangers in need. Over the years they have helped many lonely students and others in need. Somehow abused wives, disturbed children, and neglected teenagers from the social housing area close to their church building, hear of them and come for help and comfort."

Melvyn and Immanuel left the house amid the loud chatter and laughter at the dinner table.

"Again you see the kingdom advancing in the actions of my people, as they are prepared for serving and accepting service, with delight, in my Father's kingdom. The work of the kingdom in the lives of my people in this world will not be lost, or count for nothing. Through their actions they become the people they will be, and their good works will be part of who they become. Their beautiful characters are being honed for the next life. My kingdom advances day by day and hour by hour."

In no time they were in the heart of a huge city teaming with the poor and desperate. When anyone who seemed affluent appeared in the streets, children surrounded them grabbing at their clothes, and begging for money. Many others, people too old, too sick, or too disabled to get up, lay on dirty mats by the roadside holding out baskets for alms. A young man with a couple of helpers was talking to some of the young beggars. They seemed to quieten down as he talked, and a few of them began to follow him. Melvyn followed the motley band to buildings on the outskirts of the city. Here some older teenagers appeared with food, smiles, and eager talk. After eating, the ragged band was escorted around the simple facilities of the complex while a guide explained the rules of the organization. In one building, the young man they had first seen began explaining the good news of the love of God, and the inclusion of every human in that love. He explained that since God is our creator, he is the one who keeps us alive in himself, even although we all rebelled against him and brought untold misery into the world. He went on to explain the character and work of Immanuel, how he had become a human like us, how he had taken on himself the sin of the world and dealt it a death blow, in his own death. He told them the good news that Immanuel, through the power of God, had been raised from the dead. He was now seated in glory in heaven, praying for all who trust in him. He promised his followers that he would always be with them, although they would not be able to see him, and that he would come again to this world to set up a wonderful new kingdom where there would be love and justice, and more than enough of everything good for everyone. In him alone every human being can have the hope of a better future when he comes again. The children were invited to stay and become disciples of Immanuel, or they were free to return to the streets if they so wished. Some of the newcomers left while others chose to stay.

"Here again is the work of the kingdom, with the good news being preached to the poor," Immanuel observed as he again joined Melvyn. "This work will never be forgotten or lost. This caring mind-set fits right into the kingdom, and this love will flourish on in the renewed earth."

Next the pair came to a beautiful old town. Some kind of demonstration was taking place. People were marching into the town square carrying placards in a script and language Melvyn could not read. Their faces were grave but non-threatening. Apparently they were calling for the reform of their government, and an end to the brutal dictatorship that had enslaved them for many years.

Melvyn watched horrified as trucks sped into the square and soldiers jumped out and began shooting into the ranks of the peaceful demonstrators. Dead and wounded were left on the streets, while those leading the march were carted off in trucks. Once the soldiers had gone, relatives and friends began to emerge from the side streets to tend the dying, and remove the dead. Wails and shrieks of grief pierced the air as loved ones were identified and taken to hospital, or if beyond help, to a make-shift mortuary.

For hours, weary doctors and nurses at the nearby hospital fought hard to save lives and alleviate pain. As night approached a convoy of soldiers arrived at the hospital, dragged off some of the doctors and nurses into trucks, and roughed up anyone who dared protest. Outside in the dark shots were heard. Seeking revenge a sizeable army of militant protesters had acquired weapons and ambushed the soldiers, killing some and injuring others. With screeching tires the soldiers sped off, leaving their dead and injured colleagues on the street, where they had fallen. As soon as they were gone, the remaining staff carried the wounded soldiers into the hospital, and tended them just as gently and carefully as they had earlier tended the wounded demonstrators.

"I'm sure I'd leave them to die in the street," Melvyn hissed indignantly.

"That's not the way of my kingdom," Immanuel rebuked softly. "My people do not fight evil with evil."

"But they butchered the demonstrators for no reason, and carted off the doctors and nurses, who were only trying to save lives," Melvyn shouted.

"Would maltreating the soldiers stop the bloodshed? Surely the only thing likely to touch such hard hearts is showing love and goodness? My people do not fight darkness with darkness," Immanuel replied with a sigh.

"Maybe there's wisdom in what you say. I begin to see what you are getting at," Melvyn replied thoughtfully.

Next Melvyn was brought to an old house set in eleven acres of gardens and forest. Lush plants festooned the deck where a woman was sitting reading. A bowl of beans and rice lay within reach, on a small table beside her. The telephone rang and she went inside to answer it. Her voice could be heard as she brought the receiver out to the deck.

"Just reading and tucking into my beans and rice for the sixth dinner in a row," she said. A moment later she added, "It's to save money, so that I can give as much as possible to the fund to get my pastor's new book published."

"I hope this pastor is eating beans and rice night after night to help get his own book published," Melvyn observed sceptically.

"That is not Rose's concern. She is doing this for me, so that the good news can reach as many people as possible. She herself has been greatly blessed through the teaching of this man, and she will not lose her reward. I look at the intents of the heart, at the sacrifice she is making, and at her love for me and the Gospel. She is part of my advancing kingdom."

At their next port of call beans and rice did not look so bad. An impossibly gaunt woman was struggling to lift an emaciated child from the roadside. They watched as she carried the child a hundred yards down the road and laid him by the dusty roadside. She returned to the three other children she had left behind, and repeated the task until all four children were reunited. Once more she set off with a child too weak to walk or protest, on her hip, and took him another hundred yards down the road.

"She has been on the road three days already. After one day the youngest child could no longer walk and she carried him. Next day the other three children succumbed, and for a day and a half she has persevered in this arduous task of taking her children to the nearest aid centre for food. All her food and almost all her water has gone," Immanuel explained.

A dusty truck rumbled into sight and stopped beside the woman and her children. Too exhausted to speak and with tears streaking her cheeks, she allowed herself and her children to be lifted into the back of the truck. Friendly arms cradled her, gave her and her children some water, while the truck was turned around to take them quickly to the aid centre.

"The love and sacrifice of that woman shows a heart reflecting mine, and ripe for the full life of the kingdom. She will get no rewards or medals in this life, but such brave people are the great ones in my kingdom. I love her so much," Immanuel continued.

"Will she even survive?" Melvyn asked perplexed.

"Life is never going to be easy for her. She is going to survive and her children are going to survive, through the relentless efforts of more of my servants. They are greatly beloved and none of them toil in vain," Immanuel answered.

"But I know many have died in this famine already, Immanuel. How can you say none of their labour is in vain?" Melvyn queried.

"The life of the kingdom is here. It began with my resurrection and will soon be complete. Only through death will humans pass on to full life in my kingdom. A day is coming when all greed and injustice, all indifference and selfishness will be judged, a day when all wrongs will be righted. This is not the end. This is just the beginning, the rebirth of the hearts and minds of my people to be followed by their resurrection into new bodies, into a new world, and the coming of heaven to earth."

"Can all wrongs done from the beginning of time really be righted?" Melvyn asked in unbelief. "Can you really do this? If you have the power then why do you let such injustice go unpunished? Do you really care about what is happening now?"

"Do I care? Am I not the God whose essence is love? Do I not know what it is to be treated unjustly? Do I not know what it feels like to be tortured and killed? Do I not still bear the scars in my body? I did not wreck the universe. I did not make people evil. I gave humanity free will. They have done and continue to do this to themselves, but I have carved out a way through the darkness, the folly, the blood and the hell of destruction, to recreation, justice, peace, and life indeed. My kingdom has begun and will come, and my will shall be done on earth as it is in heaven. I died with humanity to kill off sin, and rose again with them to give new life to those dead in sin and misery. Do I care?"

Melvyn trembled and dared say no more. Immanuel's indignation and passion enveloped Melvyn, and almost choked him. He felt his legs wobble and buckle under him until Immanuel reached out and caught him. His strength returned immediately.

Their next visit was again to one of poverty but also of joy. A young woman was reading to a large family seated around a fire, in a primitive house. The dark eyes of the children shone with anticipation and the parents listened enraptured, as the young woman read and explained the allegory of the pilgrim's progress to the kingdom. Love flooded from the woman's eyes as she looked up from her reading and laughed. She was filled again with wonder, not only at the glory of the news she was bringing them, but the joy of knowing that the message was finding a foothold, in the Spirit prepared hearts of the family before her.

"Week by week Jane comes and reads to this family. It is the highlight of their week and of Jane's too, as she shares in my joy when someone responds to my love. The powers that be, in this country, would send her back to her own country if they knew what she was doing. They do not allow their citizens to change their religion. Jane prefers to obey my Spirit, rather than the repressive powers of an evil government, that will not allow its citizens to embrace the truth, and so enjoy life in me. Meanwhile her husband is doing great work translating Scriptures into the native language of the people. Soon the people here will be able to read Scripture for themselves. When that happens and when my word is unleashed, the people of this country will come flooding into the kingdom."

Melvyn was intrigued.

Melvyn was taken to see a doctor taking medicine from Christians in a more affluent land, to people too poor to buy even antibiotics to cure their septic cuts, chest infections, and other relatively uncomplicated medical problems.

In quick succession they went on to see many ordinary people showing kindness, caring, and building one another up in their lives and faith. Helping hands appeared alleviating suffering in fire, flood, tornadoes, volcanic eruptions, blizzards, and other disaster situations. Kind words were uttered in bereavement, sickness, sorrow, and forgiveness was shown after betrayal, injustice, gossip, and broken promises.

"Now to one of my favourite incidents," said Immanuel taking Melvyn on board a naval vessel. A young sailor had just then been wrongly accused of being the ring leader who had taken a group of recruits on shore for the evening, and allowed them to miss curfew. In fact he had been on board ship all evening. The captain meted out punishment to the whole group, but he reserved the severest punishment for the one he considered was most to blame for the incident.

"Lewis, you can clean out all the latrines and you'd better do a good job of it," he barked.

The young sailor changed clothes and made his way to the ship's toilets. The putrid smell reached him before he ever got inside the room, as he knew it would.

Nobody ever seemed to think of cleaning the toilets. That job seemed to be reserved as a punishment, and was performed with the greatest reluctance by surly offenders. Lewis was now wearing overalls and carrying the cleaning equipment he would need. He stopped just inside the door. He had already decided what he was going to do. He looked around at the filth, lime scale, tarnished brass fittings and paused to pray, "Lord you know I don't deserve this punishment but it is pointless to protest my innocence. Please give me the strength and ability to clean these filthy toilets as they have never been cleaned before."

The young man got to work. He hacked and scrubbed and mopped and polished till the brass shone, the toilets gleamed, and the floors and walls came up a colour nobody remembered. He washed carefully, got into his clean naval uniform, and reported that he had completed his task. The captain went to inspect his work and shook his head as he looked around.

"Lewis, you are something else! What can I say? You have done a superb job. No wonder the lads look up to you. See you don't lead them into mischief another time."

"This man is one of mine. He puts into practice my words to be wise as serpents and harmless as doves. He goes the second mile. The first mile was what was expected of him, cleaning the toilets as his captain had ordered. The second mile was his service to God, getting the toilets as clean as he possibly could. His wisdom earned his captain's respect, and later on his friendship for the rest of his life, so that eventually the truth could be heard and Lewis' innocence was believed.

This incident took place many years ago but my kingdom is expanding day by day and hour by hour, like yeast in a batch of dough. To most people the spread of the kingdom is invisible. The clamour of evil and the subtle twisting by the media of reported events to make them more sensational, bombard the minds and eyes of people every day. Lives are blighted by lies and slander. A little spark sets a great forest alight. Evil is rampant and destructive, but my kingdom is advancing and we will allow nothing to thwart our plans for a new heaven and a new earth.

Adam and Eve ate of the forbidden fruit from the tree of the knowledge of good and evil, and their children are still eating of that fruit today. Every day the knowledge of good and evil is crying out from every human, every family, every land, and the whole universe is groaning with the pain of it. By the time my kingdom is fully come, my kingdom inhabitants will be so inoculated against the depravity of evil, that their very beings will yearn for wholeness, for service, for generosity, for peace, and for everything good. Evil will have no foothold in them ever again.

From before time we set boundaries that were determined by who we are. Our character, our essence is love. In love we forgive, in love we change or destroy all evil. Even in wrath we are wholly holy love. Whatever the cost, the creation will be good again. We made humanity in our image, and to our image they will be fully restored.

Melvyn, I sense you have another question?"

"I do. I'm still bothered about where all the evil comes from in spite of your death and resurrection. Paul wrote about being prevented by the Satan from going places and doing things. Why is evil still so strong?" Melvyn asked.

"At the cross evil hit rock bottom, Melvyn. It was all gathered together, individual, societal, political, demonic, and all the powers of darkness in the world of humans and the heavenly realms, powers of chaos and death, came to put the Son of God to death. They believed they had triumphed when they saw me dying on a Roman cross, but they had no idea that my death was the instrument for their own destruction. They are the ones dying now and they know it. They are defeated and they know the Day of Judgement is coming; so they are determined to wreck as much havoc on my kingdom before that day, as they possibly can. They do not seem, in their mad fury, to realize that my Father can turn their worst acts against them, and rescue our children refined from out of their clutches."

"But the thing is they are not always rescued," Melvyn protested.

"Melvyn, you are thinking as if your present life is the only life. Everything is going to be put right in the end, and those hurt and killed for my sake will be rescued. Meanwhile I am always with my people no matter what they have to endure, or how they are tempted."

"Does the Satan do things we cannot see as humans?" Melvyn asked. "Is he ever able to use believers to do his dirty work? You see, it seems to me that Christians are often as bad as or worse, than unbelievers. I have heard of situations in churches where Christians have lied about and slandered other Christians, ruining their reputations, and depriving them of their ability to work. Often unbelievers seem much kinder and more loving than Christians. How can this be?"

"You are right, Melvyn. The Satan and his malevolent forces sometimes embed themselves in individuals to block our purposes, and hold them up for a while, but if we give the devils enough rope they usually hang themselves. It is a truly terrible thing for one of mine to open themselves, or their organisation, to being used by evil forces in such a way. Anyone who stretches out a hand against one of mine, especially one of my Gospel messengers, is touching the apple of my eye and will not go unscathed, but in escaping will do so as through a scorching fire. Yet it is only for a time, until the Gospel has reached all nations, and all people, that this state of affairs will be allowed to continue. My people are called to implement my victory, and to give themselves to living in my powerful love. In this way they advance my kingdom and become fit to live in it."

Melvyn found himself sitting again on the grassy bank beside the stream. Immanuel seemed to have gone. He thought of Lucifer, the brilliant angel who rebelled against his maker and became the enemy of all that is good. Hurled out of heaven, God's dwelling place, he took other angels with him and together they embraced all that is evil and anti-God. No good is left in them, but only a spirit of evil and darkness. Melvyn thought of the names and acts of the Satan recorded in the Bible: the accuser, the father of lies, the tempter, a snake, a dragon, the prince of the power of the air, who tempts humans to do evil, deceives humans, teaches false doctrine through humans, binds humans in sickness, invades humans to the point of madness, and one who is always on the prowl looking out for strays, and anyone he can devour. There is indeed nothing good left in him, none of his previous light, but only evil and darkness. Eventually he will be expelled to outer darkness which is his odious choice. Melvyn shuddered and woke up in hospital again.

Chapter Thirteen

Melvyn goes Home

Thursday afternoon Melvyn was released home into Angelina's care, with a strict pain and aftercare regimen. Karen avoided talking to Angelina, kissed her father goodbye, and made her way home with grave misgivings.

Adam and the kids were delighted to see her, and their banter soon took precedence over her misgivings. As Adam confided later she had done all she could, and worrying now was counterproductive. At dinner Adam and the kids joined her in praying for her father's recovery. She became calmer and realized how very tired she was. As soon as the children were in bed she made for hers, and slept deeply until morning.

Saturday Adam drove Karen and the kids the hundred miles to check on Melvyn. Angelina was out but Melvyn looked somewhat better. They made him comfortable, tidied and cleaned his room, and left before Angelina got back. They promised to return the following weekend, and Karen made him promise to call her if he felt worse or needed her again. He thanked her profusely for coming.

"That must be one of the very few times my father has really thanked me for anything," Karen whispered happily to Adam. "I believe he really meant it."

The following Monday Angelina returned to work. Melvyn heard the door close. Alone at home at last he gazed out through the large picture windows, across the lawn and out to the sea. He knew what he wanted to do once he heard the car start to life and drive away.

Meanwhile he stared out at the mesmerizing waves, the spray on the rocks, and the foam rolling up the sand in the bay. Forever and forever, century after century, long before he was born and no doubt long after he died the restless tide would come and go, ever obedient to the pull of the moon. It joined continent to continent, shore to shore, taking people to people, or not, as its fickle moods dictated. How quickly the might of its waters changed from calm waves on sandy shores where children and adults played and swam, to swelling raging seas that swamped and broke huge ships as easily as it did little boats. The number of its dead lying on the ocean floors was beyond counting. Did Immanuel create this vastness or did it just happen? Melvyn's dreams had been too vivid, too real to ignore. He had changed, and he had to find out if there was any substance to what he had dreamed, or if it was it all due to a passing delirium.

As soon as he heard the car drive away he threw the rug from his lap, grabbed his walking frame and purposefully made his way to his study. Among the shelves was a section devoted to world religions. There he found a slim, leather bound volume of the Holy Bible. His fretful mother had given him the beautiful volume years before, when he was leaving home for university. He had long since discarded the volume he had read daily, at that time, and for a year or so afterwards. He no longer believed the contents, but he hung on to his mother's copy as he still believed no educated adult should be ignorant of the contents of the Bible. After all, it had shaped much of western civilization and references and allusions popped up regularly in literature, and in other places. With his background he knew more of its contents than most people did, but a different goal now motivated his interest in perusing this book. He had to find out if the God he had met in his dreams bore any resemblance to the God of the Bible. Certainly the God he had been brought up to believe in was nothing like Immanuel. Yet had not a voice in his dreams told him that the judgemental, unrelenting God his parents proclaimed and modelled was a false god, and nothing like the one true God.

He reached for the volume and trundled back to his couch by the window. Before lunch he had read quickly through the first three Gospels. The story of the Messiah was familiar. His birth, life, death, resurrection, and ascension were as he had remembered them. Yet there was so much he had missed in his youth. He never really paid close attention to the message the Messiah proclaimed, nor indeed to the message John, the Baptist, had also proclaimed about Christ. He read how John the Baptist had preached that people should turn from sin and towards God, in preparation for the coming king, and life in his kingdom. When John saw the Spirit descend on Christ after his baptism, he shouted in joy to everyone that that was the sign he had been told to look out for, and that this man was indeed the Messiah, the Lamb of God who was taking away the sin of the world. John was the son of a priest and his birth was regarded

as miraculous, with prophesies about him becoming the
one who would prepare the way for the Messiah. His
family, being from a priestly heritage, was well known
and people all over the country had heard the
circumstances of his birth, giving rise to speculations
and hopes for his future. That was why, when he began
his ministry, even the Scribes and Pharisees came out to
hear him and be baptized by him.

Talk of the coming of the Messiah was on everyone's
lips as they were under the yoke of Rome, and everyone
longed for the day when God would remember his
Covenant with Abraham and bring freedom and glory
to his chosen people, as in the days of David and
Solomon. They looked for their enemies to be defeated
by a son of David, and for God's kingdom to come with
Israel being the light of the nations, and the Gentiles
bringing tribute to them instead of them having to pay
taxes to the hated Romans. They had questioned John
closely to understand whether he himself might be the
Messiah. John pointed to Jesus and told them that Jesus
was the Messiah. Jesus later used the priests' and elders'
belief that John was a prophet, and yet their refusal to
believe John's witness to himself being the Messiah, to
show up the hypocrisy of their animosity towards him.
They could not logically believe that John was a true
prophet come from God, and at the same time deny
John's message that Jesus was the Messiah.

Jesus preached the same message about the kingdom
as John had, but that it had already began. He also
showed them in words and deed what the kingdom
would be like when it had fully come, and what kind of
king he was going to be. The message of the Gospels
was the message of the coming kingdom, and both John

and Jesus proclaimed it. It was God's plan for his good but now spoiled creation.

Early in his ministry Jesus had shown promise of becoming the kind of Messiah the Jewish leaders and people all wanted, and expected. Jesus healed the sick, opened the eyes of the blind, opened the ears of the deaf, cleansed lepers, made the lame walk, miraculously fed the multitudes, and preached with authority. Surely he, the same as Elijah, could call down fire on their enemies and usher in the kingdom they all longed for. Several times they tried to take him by force and make him king but he always slipped away from them. He was not going to become the kind of king they were expecting their Messiah to be. No wonder when he entered Jerusalem to their shouts of "Hosanna to the son of David!" and their waving of branches, their expectations reached fever pitch. No wonder the following week his lack of action, as they saw it, dashed their hopes to bits. They were then more than ready to have him crucified, as a bogus Messiah who deceived the people.

Melvyn's father seldom preached from the Gospels. Melvyn could not remember him ever preaching on the kingdom, though he did use the parables and miracles to warn his congregation of their need to repent and be ready for the Day of Judgment. Mostly his preaching had emphasized sin and God's holiness, and his just anger with unrepentant sinners. Melvyn often had the impression from his father's sermons, that God the Father was so angry with sinners that he was in two minds whether to send them straight to hell as punishment, or forgive them. Jesus had to persuade a reluctant Father, it seemed, to accept Christ's torture and death, as a stand-in sacrifice to appease the Father's wrath, and pay the price for sin. God, the Father, was just and had to punish sin. He had to give Christ a severe punishment on the cross, and kill him to satisfy his just anger, and look favourably on sinners. Melvyn had often wondered how one God could be one God, and yet be at such odds within himself, in his dealings and attitude towards sinners. The Father and the Son did not seem to be of the same mind when it came to their attitude to sinners.

Melvyn's father's texts were usually from Romans and Galatians. He did preach about a life after death, but it was a going to heaven for believers and a going to hell for non-believers. Heaven was a spiritual realm of bliss of a very unearthly kind. It was not a life on a renewed earth that bore any resemblance to the present physical earth, even if he did sometimes mention a renewed heaven and a renewed earth. His father also seemed to get a strange pleasure from expanding on the tortures of hell. This, in turn, seemed to rouse the emotions of his congregation as few other subjects did. They took his firm stance on the unending tortures of hell as proof of his orthodoxy. His eloquence on the pleasures of heaven was very much more muted. Melvyn had actually been secretly afraid that heaven would be rather a dull place, perhaps resembling a never ending church service like the ones his father conducted. Naturally even that would be preferable to hell where sinners burned but never died, in white hot flames. He contented himself with hoping for a long interesting life first, and then life in heaven after death, as the lesser of two evils. His father's heaven bore little or no resemblance to the kingdom life Immanuel had shown Melvyn.

For lunch Melvyn sat at the kitchen table and ate a small sandwich and half a tub of yogurt, but he felt very weak. He had very little appetite though he knew he had to eat a little and often, as he had been instructed, to get what remained of his stomach to expand to cope with sufficient food to keep healthy. He had also been told he needed to gain weight as he had lost a lot of weight. After eating as much as he could, he decided to have a nap on the couch but to set an alarm to waken himself after a couple of hours. He wanted to leave himself enough time to read the Gospel of John, plus John's Epistles, and maybe even Revelation, before Angelina came home. He did not yet feel confident enough to face her scorn should she find him reading the Bible. In any case, there was no sense in antagonizing her at this point, should he later find the whole experience had been an illusion. It would be time enough to tell her, if he ever got to the point of believing even half of what he had dreamed and read.

He slept deeply until awakened by the alarm. He went to the bathroom, then made a cup of coffee and took his pain medications and a little food. He settled down to read John's Gospel. He stopped at verse three of the first chapter and mulled it over. It was so in tune with what the Holy Spirit had said in his dream. Every last thing was made by Immanuel, and Immanuel was the source of all life. According to John nothing existed without Immanuel creating it. As the Holy Spirit had said every breath a human takes comes from him, and he supposed every atom and every part of every atom in every element, was held together by Immanuel. She had also said that when Christ died all humanity died with him. He needed to become a human to die, and yet he remained God at the same time. He held and holds all humanity in himself, and their life so depends on his that when he died they died too, in union with him, to sever forever the hold of sin and death on them. Then when he rose, they rose with him to new life. Their fate, she had said, was united to his in life, in death, in resurrection, and even in the life to come. People have no life in themselves. All life is derived from Christ.

He read on about the Father who sent the Son into the world, because he loved humanity so much he was determined to rescue them from the awful ravages of sin. He read about the Holy Spirit who anointed Messiah for the task, and brought humanity to new birth in the resurrection of Messiah. He remembered one time being puzzled about that when he was reading the Epistle of Peter. It now made sense. Humanity has been reborn through Christ's resurrection from the dead, though those unaware of, or resisting this truth, are to all extent and purposes blind and dead. They do not live in this reality because they cannot hear or are not listening to the Spirit's promptings to believe the truth, although she is speaking to them continually. Unless people embrace the truth that God is for them, they are not free to be changed and prepared for the life of the coming kingdom. Union with Christ has to translate into communion with Christ for this change to occur. Melvyn realised that in a dark, unenlightened state, people would actually experience life in the new kingdom as hell. God cannot and will not allow such people to enter the kingdom and spoil it.

He read on. How soon the authorities began to be jealous of the crowds Jesus attracted to hear his message, and how soon they began to find fault with him. They did not like his popularity and they did not like the fact that he did not adhere to the orthodox interpretations of the Torah, the Law, as they saw it. They had become so tied up in the Torah, and the Temple rituals that were supposed to help them recognize Messiah when he came, that they could no longer see the goal of the Torah and the Temple rituals. They could no longer see them as only temporary signposts, pointing them to greater realities. The Torah and the Temple became an end in themselves, and they received the honour and worship due the Messiah. The Messiah himself they began to hate.

Melvyn could now see the absolute centrality of the Messiah being the one who made and sustains everything. He could never save his people unless he could bring them down into death, as only death would put their sin to death. Melvyn quickly skimmed over to the Epistles and found in Colossians and Hebrews the same stress on the Messiah as the creator, and the one who sustains the universe. This made sense of the death of Christ to deal with sin. The Triune God was of one mind in seeking to save humanity by the only means possible. Melvyn was amazed at the love of the Father in giving his Son over to death for humanity, to rescue them from evil.

Melvyn's mind wandered. He tried to work things out from what he had read. He thought of the big plan God had for creation before anything had come into existence. Adam and Eve were made in the image of God. When God looked at them he could see himself, as people see themselves in a mirror. Sin shattered that mirror and God could no longer see much of himself in that shattered mirror.

Eat of that tree and you will die God had told them. Yet, before they were even created, God had a plan that encompassed that death, in the death of his Son. The plan would deal with sin, defeat death and bring about the recreation and new birth of humanity, and the whole universe. The One who sustains life would die and so everything would die with him. John the Baptist saw Christ as God's lamb who takes away the sin of the world. The allusion, of course, was to the Passover lamb that was killed and its blood daubed over the door posts of the Israelites' homes in Egypt, so that the Angel of Death would spare the lives of those within. The lamb had to die. He knew that the reference in the Old Testament to the "life being in the blood," and the prohibition against eating or drinking blood, was a way of referring to life and death. When the New Testament talked of the shedding of Christ's blood, or the cleansing power of Christ's blood, it was another way of referring to the efficacy of his death in destroying sin and death.

To die Christ had to become human, and for his resurrection and ascension to be effective for humanity Christ had to remain human and he had to remain God. Only God the Creator could hold every life past, present, and future, in himself. The death of humans, their sin and every ill effect of the shattered mirror, he would bring down into death, killing off sin forever. He became sin and took the curse of sin, death, on himself in his death. Since he was God and a sinless human being as well, death had no power to keep holding on to him. Once Messiah had accomplished his goal of dealing with sin, he then carried humanity still in union with himself, on to resurrection and ascension. No mere human could do this. Every human being owes total loving obedience to the Creator, and total loyalty to him in every situation. Perfection is the standard required to continue in a right relationship with God. Even if one could save oneself, one could in no way save any other sinful human being. One's perfection would only be sufficient for oneself, and not an iota more. Such perfection is, of course, only theoretical. Ever since the Fall of mankind perfection is impossible for any ordinary fallen human being, as experience has proved time after time. Messiah's life of sinless perfection was an essential part of the total saving gift of grace to humanity. Only through Messiah's sinless life, in a substitute capacity gifted to humanity, could perfection be achieved.

"Hold on!" Melvyn thought. "This won't do. Death is not finished. Disease, my cancer, is very real. This does not make sense."

He stared out of the window again at the restless sea. His mind was overloaded and he felt very tired. He hid the Bible under a cushion, lay back and closed his eyes. He really should get up and take a little walk out on the terrace, as the doctor had advised, but he felt too tired.

The phone rang. It was Karen. They talked for a while and then she asked him if he had walked outside at all. She advised him to do so, and he promised her that he would. He felt stronger after talking to her, and he did indeed go outside with the aid of his walking frame. He reached the edge of the terrace and sat down on the stone bench that looked over the lawn and down to the sea. He breathed the fresh salty air and sighed deeply. He felt confused. Eventually he made his way back inside and began to mull things over again.

"Immanuel doesn't want puppets for friends," a voice unbidden whispered in his head. He thought about that. He remembered that Immanuel had said that to him. People had to go through some of the consequences of the Fall, to experience for themselves the ugliness and horror of being out of alignment with their Maker. They had to know something of what they were being freed from. They had to learn to hate even the appearance of evil. Immanuel had talked about their minds being renewed, and even inoculated against evil. Those who are forgiven much love much, but only if they realize how much they have been forgiven. People need to be trained for kingdom life. If they were just zapped into compliance it would not involve a real choice on their part. For God to see himself again in the mirror of humanity, the mirror has to be remade. God is real, and he wants humanity to image his reality of love and joy and everything good.

The door opened in the middle of his reverie. Angelina was home, and he would have to put his thoughts and readings on hold until he had some privacy again.

Chapter Fourteen

Visiting Paul's World

Unexpectedly, after dinner (he had managed to eat some scrambled egg and a few crackers) Angelina went out to a book reading club, and Melvyn was able to retrieve his Bible and resume his reading.

Jesus' teachings in the Gospel of John were similar to those in the other Gospels, Melvyn had found. Christ showed the people by word and deed that he truly was the Messiah, though not the kind of Messiah they were looking for, or even wanted. They wanted a Messiah who would rescue the nation of Israel by force, and give them the kingdom. Instead Jesus showed them in sermon after sermon, through illustration after illustration from the Old Testament Scriptures, that the promised Messiah and his kingdom would not fight darkness with darkness. His kingdom would be one of love, justice, peace, and true holiness. He talked of being the good shepherd, the bread of life, the door, the light of the world, the water of life, the way, the truth, and the life.

He claimed to be intimately acquainted with God the Father. He promised his disciples that he would send his

Holy Spirit to his people, when he himself left earth to take his throne at the Father's right hand, after his ascension. He even claimed that through the Holy Spirit, he and his Father would indwell believers. He promised that he would always be with his people and that he would come again to take them to be with himself, in the kingdom of the age to come. His death, resurrection, appearances, and instructions to his apostles and disciples were as Melvyn remembered them from his younger days, when he read the Bible daily, only now they were more real to him.

He skipped on to the Epistles of John. He read John's stress on the deity of Christ and how he urged his readers to keep in fellowship with the Trinity, and with each other. That fellowship, of course, was one of pure love, and believers were always to walk in the light of the Messiah's love, and in obedience to their Lord. John he finds is cognizant of the fact that though this will be the characteristic walk of the believers, they will on occasion sin. They will need to repent and get back into walking in the light as quickly as possible, always assured of the cleansing forgiveness of their God. John warns them of the plots of the Evil One, who will try to lure them away by listening to wrong teachings and by other means, such as lust and worldly ambition. They must continue faithfully walking in love, living always in union with Christ, and under the guidance of his Holy Spirit. The Holy Spirit is the one who will continually help them to live by faith, and faith will express itself in love.

Melvyn remembered the amazing love that engulfed him in his kingdom dreams. John was urging believers to live in the reality of that love even in this world, before its complete renewal. That must be what Immanuel meant by showing him the examples of people who were being prepared for kingdom life, and who were living it in the present time.

Melvyn sat back and sighed deeply. Was it all pie in the sky? Why was he so drawn to this too good to be true way of living? He remembered how alive he had felt with Immanuel. He remembered the energy, the joy, the acceptance that seemed to bounce to him from every person there, from the animals, and even from the bubbling stream in Immanuel's kingdom. He thought of Immanuel's treatment of him. It was real and yet there was no condemnation of him, only acceptance. There was no pretence that his behaviour did not matter or that sin was acceptable. Immanuel's love was a burning, cleansing love. It was a white hot light that left nowhere to hide, without a word being uttered. It searched the thoughts and intents of Melvyn's heart. Guile, excuses, equivocations, deceit, scuttled away like insects looking to escape when a rock is turned over. From Immanuel's eyes, from his words, from his body language, all was love. His love had enfolded Melvyn and though it had also showed him himself in a way he had never before admitted, even to himself, Melvyn was drawn to this terrifying purity. He wanted Immanuel's wholeness. He wanted Immanuel's wholesomeness. He wanted to be clean and pure and free and beautiful. He wanted to become loving.

He now began to understand what Immanuel had said about his love for Stella. He had not loved Stella with Immanuel's love. Then a voice inside his head argued. How could he? She was not always very nice. She often found Melvyn's behaviour irritating and told him so. He smiled ruefully at himself. That was the difference between himself and Immanuel. Immanuel loved him, even although he was anything but nice. Immanuel's love did not depend on Melvyn's behaviour being attractive. Immanuel's love was constant and could not be changed or influenced by anything Melvyn did. Melvyn realized it was a healing love, a forgiving love, a perfecting love, an unchangeable love that changed Melvyn and made him want to be part of that wonderful kingdom, where nobody was looking out for number one. In that kingdom, love was the air of life and everyone lavished care, protection, gifts, time, and effort on everyone else, counting it pure joy to have their kindness and services accepted.

He had blown it with Stella, but what about Angelina? When they first met she made him feel so good. He was so in love with her; she could do no wrong and she had no faults. He thought of the vows he had made to her, to love her always come what may. Cynically, he realized now that what he had really meant was that he had loved the way she had made him feel. He wanted to marry her to give her the opportunity to make him feel that way for the rest of his life.

How soon after marrying her he had realized she was vain and shallow, untrustworthy, and utterly selfish. She spent almost all the money she earned on clothes, cosmetics, hairdressers, seaweed wraps, and cosmetic surgery. She had intellectual gifts but even these were mostly second hand. Her abilities were due mostly to a good memory, and her opinions mostly those of the latest authors she had read. How could he ever love somebody like that? How could he look at her and love every fibre of her being, knowing how flawed she was?

How could he love her with his words, his touch, and his whole being when he despised her? How could he spend time with her and enjoy her company, when they had nothing in common?

"That's not the point. Immanuel's love is not about being loved but loving," Melvyn reasoned with the voices in his head.

He thought how wonderful it would be to have a marriage where one could forget oneself and completely enfold another in love, a marriage where seeing the faults of the other did not dampen love, did not cause one to pull back and utter hurtful words of judgment and condemnation. He could not do it, not with Angelina. Things had gone too far for love to be rekindled.

Yet how did Immanuel do it? Immanuel knew what Melvyn was like, knew every rotten selfish thought in his head, knew every mean despicable thing he had ever done, and yet only love oozed from him to Melvyn. Love is as strong as death he remembered from the Song of Solomon. Immanuel had said he, Melvyn, had not loved Stella with his, Immanuel's, love. Perhaps this kind of love was a gift Immanuel gave people, like the gift of faith he was told some people had.

"It's all a lie. How could you possibly love a person like Angelina? She's not worth loving. It's too late anyway. She'll never love you again," the voices in his head flooded in raucously, dispelling his peace.

"I can't sort this out now. I'm too confused and too conflicted. I need to sort out what I believe before I can act on anything," he reasoned.

He would read on. Tomorrow he would tackle his father's favourite books, Romans and Galatians.

Next morning, as planned, Melvyn started reading Romans as soon as Angelina left for work. He read the first chapter of Romans. After Paul's greetings, his reasons for writing, his assurance of salvation for both believing Jews and Gentiles alike, he launched into the history of the destructive power of evil in the life of humanity. Listening to a created being, the Evil One, rather than to God, humanity's thinking became futile and foolish and their worship became idolatrous. They believed the Evil One's lies, and God let them have their own way. He left them to discover where that would lead them. Their wrong thinking led inevitably to wrong behaviour, and wrong behaviour inevitably led to their dehumanization.

As he read the catalogue of evil which resulted from people suppressing the knowledge of God and doing their own thing, Melvyn remembered his vision of hell. It was as Paul described in the letter to the Romans: "Since they didn't bother to acknowledge God, God quit bothering them and let them run loose. And then all hell broke loose: rampant evil, grabbing and grasping, vicious backstabbing. They made life hell on earth with their envy, wanton killing, bickering, and cheating. Look at them: mean-spirited, venomous, fork-tongued God-bashers. Bullies, swaggers, insufferable windbags! They keep inventing new ways of wrecking lives. They ditch their parents when they get in the way. Stupid, slimy, cruel, cold-blooded."

So far he could follow the logic of the book but when he got to the second chapter confusion hit. The argument of the book changed from evil deeds recorded in the third person, to ones recorded in the second person. Who was this "you" Paul was addressing whose, "Judgmental criticism of others is a well-known way of escaping detection in your own crimes and misdemeanors"?

The chapter went on railing at this evil person, and comparing him with someone who does what is good. Paul seemed to have left salvation through faith in Christ behind, at this point, and to be preaching a Gospel of condemnation for evil doers, and of blessing for those who did right. Where did this leave what he had said in the first chapter, about the sufficiency of faith in Christ for salvation? Then more confusing still, he started railing at Jews who boast of having and keeping the law. He accuses them of blatantly breaking the law. Melvyn read on but in confusion and utter frustration he eventually gave up. He was utterly at a loss. This made no sense at all. No wonder his father had such a horrible threatening picture of God. If Paul was right God said one thing one minute and the opposite the next. First it was all forgiveness and love and good news, and then next outright condemnation, judgment, and wrath. He put the Bible down and held his head in his hands.

"Immanuel, what can I do? I don't understand this at all. I need your Spirit to show me the meaning of this terrible book!"

No sooner had Melvyn prayed than a picture of the Reverend Robert Thomas came unbidden into his mind. Reverend Thomas was the hospital chaplain Melvyn had dismissed from his bedside, rather rudely, less than a month earlier. Melvyn was due to return to the hospital for a check-up the following day.

Perhaps Reverend Thomas could help him make sense of Romans or suggest some commentaries he might read. He put the Bible back under the cushion and after eating and having a rest, he decided to trundle outside to the stone seat, to clear his mind.

The afternoon air was warm, calm, and faintly scented from the flowers and bushes that bordered the terrace. He could see and hear the waves breaking rhythmically on the beach below, and rolling up the sand. The occasional gull or other bird flew over the water or landed on a rock. A scatter of neighbours strolled down the gently sloping path to the beach, some walking their dogs. The lawn spread out towards the path which was to the right of the house, and which was bordered by low bushes. The distance made it difficult for anyone to speak to him, but a few folks waved to him. Melvyn was feeling somewhat stronger, and he remained outdoors for almost an hour enjoying the mild weather and pleasant view, until his watch told him it was time for his medications.

On his way back in he walked around the terrace, with the aid of his walking frame. He examined the flower borders, stone pots, and hanging baskets all filled with lush colourful plants and flowers. A gardener tended the grounds once a week, but this had not been his day to come. Slowly Melvyn made his way inside. Angelina came home early and they had some dinner together, but she went out shortly afterwards. Melvyn felt tired. He decided to go to bed early. He looked out some clothes for the following day, before getting into bed and falling asleep almost immediately.

That night he again had a very lifelike dream but he was somehow outside it, placidly observing, led on from scene to scene but unable to participate or question his guide. He was taken to place after place and incident after incident, and was told many things. They appeared more vivid than written accounts, but as with written accounts, he could only ponder and question things in his mind. He could hear the voice of his guide, but he could not voice his questions.

His guide led him through some imposing city gates, down the main thoroughfare, and turned off into Straight Street, where he announced, "We are in the city of Damascus and my name is Paul." This Paul had only the vaguest resemblance to the Paul he had seen in Immanuel's land.

Paul stopped at one of the houses and said, "This is the house where I stayed, after I was blinded by Messiah's glory, as I was on my way to capture the leaders of the churches here. My mission was to take them back to Jerusalem for trial, and if things went according to my wishes, execution. How I hated the followers of Messiah, who I thought were leading my people astray. In my zeal I was out of control. I did terrible things and my very name brought fear to the believers. I was a murderous thug."

Paul opened the door and they went inside. "Here is the room where I lay for three days eating and drinking nothing, but praying and praying. I could hardly believe that I had refused to recognise the Messiah – yes, I say refused. I had seen Stephen die and the Holy Spirit was at work trying to get me to see who Jesus really was, but I was stubborn. My intellect and education, and all the teachings and traditions of our people, made me balk at the idea of a crucified Messiah. Messiah was to be the saviour of our people, ridding us of Roman occupation and setting up his everlasting kingdom in Jerusalem, while cleaning up the Temple once and for all. He would come soon and save us, if only everyone would seriously turn to God and keep Torah. I was moved by Stephen's face. It shone with an awesome glory. His message was powerful but I closed my mind to all his words, ignored my uncomfortable feelings, and instead redoubled my efforts to stamp out, what I convinced myself was a pernicious heresy.

While I was praying I saw a vision of a man called Ananias come and lay his hands on me and restore my sight. Ananias did come, and as he placed his hands on me, scales fell from my eyes and my sight was restored. At once I was filled with the Holy Spirit. I got up, was baptised, and had something to eat. I was told that I was chosen by God to carry the Gospel to the Gentiles and their rulers, and that I was to suffer greatly in the process."

Leading the way, Paul brought Melvyn to several synagogues, "This is where I began to preach that Jesus really is the Son of God. The Jews were astonished at my change of heart, almost as astonished as I was myself. Some of the believers were still afraid of me. Who could blame them? I spent many days showing the Jews from Scripture that Jesus is the Messiah, but those who did not believe plotted to kill me. They kept watch at the city gates but the believers learned of their plan, and helped me escape by letting me down over the city wall in a basket. I ran off and made my way back to Jerusalem. There I tried to join the disciples, but they too were afraid of me, suspicious of my sudden conversion. Only when Barnabas brought me to the apostles and told them my story was I accepted into the fellowship of believers, in Jerusalem.

I began preaching freely in Jerusalem and debating with the Grecian Jews, but they too rejected the message and plotted to kill me. The believers learned of their intentions and sent me off to my hometown of Tarsus. Shortly afterwards Barnabas, who had been called to help in Antioch where many Greeks had become believers through the witness of believers who had escaped from Jerusalem after the persecution that followed Stephen's death, came looking for me. He wanted me to help build up the church there which I was delighted to do. We worked together for a year and a great many people came to faith there. Indeed that's where we were first called Christians. God blessed the church with many gifts, and many believers became prophets and teachers. As we were no longer needed there the Lord sent us off to Cyprus.

You can read about all our adventures in the Book of Acts. I want to show you Ephesus, Corinth, and some of the other leading towns of Greece and Turkey where most of my preaching took place. That way you will be able to understand the different pagan cultures that were around at the time, and what we Christians were up against. Always we had the zealous Jews who were determined to keep people under the Torah restrictions, although these laws had done their job and were now fulfilled in Christ, persecuting us. Just as I had previously believed, they too thought that we were leading people astray, and that they were doing God's will by opposing us violently. However the Gentiles also opposed the Christians. Not only were many of the believers Jews (pagans never seemed to accept Jews, as they believed in only one God, and never joined in their pagan festivities and feasts), but worse we believed in a new King, and kingdom that claimed superiority over all other kings and kingdoms. Our claims about Christ coincided with a rise in the belief that Ceasar was a god, and consequently must be worshipped. Jews and Christians alike were suspected of a lack of loyalty to Ceasar because they refused to acknowledge that he was divine. If we had just been adding another god to their bevy of gods, they would have been quite happy to accept us, but our insistence that there was only one real God and that he alone was to be worshipped, and all other gods were to be renounced, provoked violent opposition to us.

All the great cities had numerous temples and shrines to every god and goddess imaginable. Religious people hardly dare move, or make a decision of any importance, without first consulting the relevant deity. They made regular sacrifices to the gods and much of the meat from the sacrifices was either eaten in the temples of the gods, which in effect became restaurants, or the surplus was sold by their priests to the marketplaces. That's why many Jews would not eat meat in these cities, and refused to eat with pagan associates, since they would almost certainly be eating food sacrificed to idols. They certainly would not go to the pagan temple restaurants to eat, as these places also housed shrine prostitutes of both sexes, and were places where black magic and fortune telling were practised.

As I said before, added to all these so-called gods the Romans had begun to worship their emperors, and in some cases even the city of Rome itself. City after city vied with one another to build fine temples to the emperors, and anyone who was a Roman citizen was entitled to eat free the meat sacrificed at these temples.

Should a citizen refuse to eat or worship at a Roman temple, question would be asked about their loyalty to Rome. The consequences for disloyalty were very serious and could involve flogging, imprisonment, and even death.

The cult of the emperors clashed with the Christian faith in other areas too. One of the titles of the emperor was 'son of god'. Julius Ceasar's adopted son had been the first emperor to declare that his father was a god. Thus he, the son of the dead emperor, became the 'son of god'".

Melvyn found himself in Rome at the top end of the Forum, under the Arch of Titus.

"Look up, Melvyn! There you can see what I mean. That carving is supposedly the soul of the emperor Titus ascending to heaven, the abode of the gods. His son claimed to be the 'son of god'. Christians believe that there is only one true God, and only Christ has the right to the title 'Son of God'. Ceasar, we believe, was a mere human.

Another title for the emperor was 'saviour of the world' who brought 'Roman peace' to the world, and whose birthday was heralded as 'good news'. Christians believe Christ saved the world from the darkness of death and evil, through reconciliation with God, and the forgiveness of sins. Angels proclaimed peace, to those who please God, to shepherds the night Jesus was born. Later the apostles and disciples were commissioned to preach the 'good news' of his resurrection, and of his coming again to bring in his new kingdom of justice, peace, and righteousness. Christians were thus undermining the claims of the emperors. At baptism, believers made the confession, 'Jesus is Lord'. That confession was a direct threat to Rome and many died for their faith."

With no interruption they found themselves in ancient Athens.

"In this city, while I was awaiting the arrival of my co-workers Timothy and Silas, I saw many of the sights which you now see around you. Just look at all the temples and shrines and statues of idol gods. It seems as if every niche has some god, every street corner a temple, and every courtyard of every house an altar," Paul lamented, "even an altar to 'TO THE GOD NOBODY KNOWS'".

Melvyn saw statues of Athena, Zeus, Apollo, Hermes, and a host of other pagan deities, in the numerous shrines and temples. They walked on to the Agora which was the hub of social, commercial, and intellectual life in Athens. In the marketplace people were selling food and wares. Around and outside the marketplace stood the covered porches, where philosophers taught. People mulled around buying and selling, but they sometimes stopped to listen, as the philosophers taught their disciples and debated with each other.

They climbed to the Acropolis and gazed in wonder at the Parthenon, with its beautifully carved exterior and grand columns. White marble friezes, some painted, decorated the outside of this breath taking building dedicated to the goddess Athena, the patron goddess of the city. Melvyn recognised some of the statues, having seen pieces of them in the British museum centuries later, though here they were in pristine condition.

In the shadow of the Acropolis, they sat in the Areopagus while Paul recapped, "I was grieved to see all this splendour around me, while the lives of the people were built on lies. They seemed to me so fraught, so empty, so hopeless, and so sad. At first I went to the synagogues to bring the good news of Jesus to my own people, and to the God-fearing Greeks who had joined them. Then I began preaching in the marketplace. It was there that the philosophers first started to debate with me. The two principal groups of philosophers in Athens were the Stoics and the Epicureans.

The Epicureans believed in the gods, but believed they were so far away as to have no interest in what people got up to. The only rational way to live, they believed, was to live as happy a life as possible because death is the end of us. They believed in the rule of law, as that prevented people hurting or getting hurt by others. They also shunned any excesses that brought pain; moderation in all things and delight in knowledge was to be treasured. Above all, the main thing was to learn to live free from the fear and superstition engendered by religion, and by the fear of death.

The Stoics on the other hand believed the gods were in charge of the affairs of men, but they were hard hearted and malevolent. Life was hard, but one could learn to live a detached life, and eventually learn to grin and bear hardships, with equanimity.

Here in a meeting of the Areopagus I was invited to explain what they saw as my new teaching, and strange ideas. The Athenians loved to debate, and the city was known far and wide for its intellectual life and love of philosophy. I acknowledged their intense religious life, and used the altar to an unknown god as my starting point. My sermon is recorded in Acts:

'It is plain to see that you Athenians take your religion seriously. When I arrived here the other day,

I was fascinated with all the shrines I came across. And then I found one inscribed, TO THE GOD NOBODY KNOWS. I'm here to introduce you to this God so that you can worship intelligently, know who you're dealing with.'"

Melvyn had been watching Paul as he spoke, when suddenly he became aware that the Areopagus was full of men, and quite a few women.

"'The God who made the world and everything in it, this Master of sky and land, doesn't live in custom-made shrines or need the human race to run errands for him, as if he couldn't take care of himself. He makes the creatures; the creatures don't make him. Starting from scratch, he made the entire human race and made the earth hospitable, with plenty of time and space for living so we could seek after God, and not just grope around in the dark but actually *find* him. He doesn't play hide-and-seek with us. He's not remote, he's *near*. We live and move in him, can't get away from him! One of your poets said it well: 'We're the God-created.' Well, if we are the God-created, it doesn't make a lot of sense to think we could hire a sculptor to chisel a god out of stone for *us*, does it?

God overlooks it as long as you don't know any better – but that time is past. The unknown is now known, and he's calling for a radical life-change. He has set a day when the entire human race will be judged and everything set right. And he has already appointed the judge, confirming him before everyone by raising him from the dead.'"

At the mention of the resurrection of the dead a great guffaw arose from the crowd, but some became very quiet and indicated to Paul that they wanted to hear more on the subject. Still others, both men and women, to Paul's delight, told him they believed his message and wanted to become disciples. A deep joy spread over Paul's face. "The Spirit is at work in the hearts of people who are willing to listen. When they hear the Gospel they embrace it with gladness. The word speaks powerfully into their souls and takes root in their lives and they are changed forever. God's word does not get lost in the wind."

Paul spoke to Melvyn again, "Nobody in the ancient pagan world of my time believed in resurrection."

Paul went on to explain, "Some believed in an afterlife, but it was a disembodied spirit life, not a fully human life such as Christ now has. That's why most of them scoffed at me when I told them Christ had been resurrected. Even among the Jews, the Sadducees did not believe in a resurrected body."

After this Paul left Athens with Melvyn, and took him to Corinth, another Greek city with strong Roman ties. Corinth was a thriving seaport and commercial centre, the crossroads of land and sea trade. It was the capital of the Roman province of Achaia which incorporated most of Greece. The cosmopolitan population comprised not only native Greeks, but retired soldiers, who had been gifted Roman citizenship and land grants for services to the emperor. There was a large contingent of Jewish and other ethnic groups, plus merchants, sailors, freedmen, slaves, and trades people. Luxuries from all over the world were bought and traded in Corinth. They were very proud of their strong Roman connections.

Looking around among the vast throng about him, Melvyn glanced up and saw the mountain that dominated the cityscape.

Paul followed his gaze and sighed, "That is Mount Acrocorinth, with the Temple of Aphrodite, the so-called goddess of love, on its summit. One thousand cult prostitutes were ready to sell themselves up there, in the name of religion. Corinth in my day was known as one of the most degenerate cities on earth, where excesses of every kind flourished and were catered to.

Though not considered as cultured as Athens, the Corinthian elite still prided themselves on their intellectual reputation, and especially the skills of their orators. As in Athens, temples, shrines, altars, and statues of gods abounded. The cult of the emperor had taken firm root in the city, and Roman citizens were entitled to eat free at the temple restaurants, on the meat sacrificed to the emperor. Magic and fortune telling, philosophers of secret knowledge, and their disciples, enticed the populace to part with their money. Yet the Lord had many people here, ready to throw off the shackles of superstition, and embrace the truth of the Gospel.

I loved the people of Corinth and the enthusiasm of their congregations. Yet the churches here gave me many sleepless nights, and we had some painful confrontations. How easy it is to be drawn into incorporating the culture of the society around, instead of following the radical new way of a crucified saviour.

Ephesus is our next port of call. There you will see more of the same as far as the culture of the day was concerned, but it was a beautiful city. Among its buildings was a magnificent temple to the goddess Artemis. The city was very wealthy when I lived there. It again was an important centre of Roman rule, and its citizens were proud of their theatres, baths, temples, and houses. Superstition and magic were rife, and many made their living from the carving of the images of the various gods and goddesses.

You will remember how when people started turning from these idols to the living God, I was accused of defaming Artemis by the silversmiths who made their living from making images of the goddess. They were finding sales from their silverware shrinking, and they wanted to be rid of us. A riot started but the proconsul knew very well that the motive of the silversmiths was mercenary, and he quickly sent them about their business. In spite of the riot and opposition there, I still have many happy memories of my time in Ephesus.

I think this gives you some idea of the forces that were at work when the church of Christ was in its infancy. From Jerusalem (yes, there were a surprising number of pagan shrines even there) out to the dispersed Jews and the Gentiles, we had to contend with idols and paganism, and the ever increasing threat from the cult of the Roman emperors. Fellow Jews were a huge problem as well because they saw us as trying to destroy the peoples' faith in the Temple, the Law, and the traditions of our nation. I should know, for I was as zealous as the best of them to stamp out the followers of the only true Messiah."

Chapter Fifteen

Melvyn gets Help from Robert

Melvyn woke early next morning. He felt he remembered only parts of his dream and he did not wish to forget anything. He jotted down some notes.

It took him a long time to get showered, shaved, and ready for his hospital appointment. When Angelina left, he helped himself to a cup of coffee and called a taxi. He decided to take his Bible and a notebook to be prepared should he be able to find Reverend Thomas. Paul had showed him some of the places he had evangelised, but Melvyn had not been able to talk to him or question him about his letters. It was interesting, and would help him understand more of the Bible, but he had a thousand questions still to be answered.

As he waited for the doctor to see him, he wrote down some of the questions that perplexed him about the Book of Romans. The doctor examined him, gave him prescriptions for more pain killers, and announced that he was healing well, if slower than expected. He would order a scan for a month hence, and on the basis of the results of the scan and blood tests, they would discuss any further treatment options that might be necessary. Melvyn shuddered inwardly at the prospects before him. He dressed and asked the aide who was helping him where he was likely to find Reverend Thomas. She kindly paged him, and came back to tell Melvyn that he could meet him in the hospital chapel.

Reverend Thomas was waiting for Melvyn at the chapel door. He obviously recognized Melvyn and remembered Melvyn's hostile dismissal of him the last time they met, but he held out his large hand and smiled in welcome.

"I suppose you never expected me to come asking for your help?" Melvyn smiled back apologetically. "I'm sorry I was so rude to you the last time we met."

"Not to worry, Mr Reed. What can I do for you?"

Melvyn briefly explained his change of heart from confirmed atheist to sceptical agnostic. Reverend Thomas listened as Melvyn shared some of his background, including his very conservative church upbringing, and his consequent rejection of the church and its teachings. Melvyn explained that because of some very lifelike dreams he had had while in hospital, he had decided to read the Bible again. He wanted to compare and contrast the teaching about God his parents had given him, with the God he had met in his dreams. He told Reverend Thomas of his relative ease in understanding the Gospels and the Epistles of John, but his utter frustration with the Book of Romans.

When Melvyn had finished speaking Reverend Thomas paused and said, "Your story is very interesting and strangely enough, not entirely dissimilar to my own. I too was brought up in a very conservative fundamentalist church. From a very early age, however, I was conscious of the presence of God in my life. It was no surprise to anyone that I decided to become a preacher and went to seminary to train.

There I became very interested in church history, and the various controversies that arose in the early church. I read the works of many of the early church fathers, the medieval mystics, the reformers, and subsequent theologians. More and more, I began to see how theologians through the ages have been influenced by the burning questions of their own day, and the philosophies of their time. The early church was influenced by Greek logic and that way of reasoning, and also by the Roman legal system current at the time. These influences continue to this day. The reformers were preoccupied with sin and the holiness of God, and as the enlightenment movement took hold, so did the power of Greek logic with its dualistic way of thinking. The prevailing culture of our own day is strongly influenced by relativistic reasoning, and a deep suspicion of any absolutes. Suffice to say that my theology evolved away from the very narrow confines of my conservative upbringing. Though I never rejected God as you did, my beliefs have been reshaped and have changed drastically over the years. God has not changed though, and I believe the Holy Spirit has been my teacher guiding me into the truth through Scripture and other means, to know more of God the Father, God the Son, and God the Holy Spirit."

Reverend Thomas paused before adding, "Romans is a very dense and hard book to understand. As with all Paul's epistles one has to understand the background to his letters. Like all theologians, Paul too was working to address errors of perception about God, and specific problems in the churches to which he was writing."

Melvyn was relieved to realize that Reverend Thomas
was intelligent and widely read. Up to now he had no
idea what Reverend Thomas believed, and for all he
knew he might be a clone of his own father, rigid and
utterly conservative in his reading of the Bible. Only the
vivid picture of Reverend Thomas coming into his mind,
when he prayed to Immanuel in his frustration over the
Book of Romans, had induced Melvyn to approach him
for help.

"So what do you see as the problem Paul was
addressing in his letter to the Roman churches?" Melvyn
asked.

"Well, we know that the Emperor Claudius had
expelled all Jews from Rome six to eight years before
Paul wrote Romans, ostensibly because of some riots.
The Romans, and indeed many people, did not like the
Jews and looked down on them. Jews did not accommodate themselves to the cultures where they settled. They
refused to eat with people of other faiths and would not
worship the local gods, or participate in pagan festivals.
Claudius died in AD 54 and the new emperor, Nero,
allowed the Jews to come back to Rome.

This meant that the Christian communities in Rome
had for several years been run by Gentile Christians,
some possibly former proselytes to the Jewish faith.
Although they were only a tiny minority of the population of Rome, maybe only four or five house churches,
they had a good reputation and standing among the
other Christian churches all over the world. Under-
standably the Roman Christians, who had taken over
the running of the churches in the absence of the expelled
Jews, would be in no mood to relinquish their way of
doing things to the returning Jews. Instructions had

filtered down to them from Jerusalem that Gentiles no longer had to undergo circumcision and keep the Torah, to be accepted as full Covenant members of Messiah's kingdom. These instructions may have led the Roman Gentile Christians to believe that God had rejected the Jews and the Torah. We can't be certain, but it seems that this is the background to the Book of Romans and a cause of friction, since the main issues being addressed are:

1) How God remains faithful to his Covenant with Abraham.
2) The place of the Torah (the Law) in the new Christian community.
3) The identity of the new Covenant Community.

Throughout the book Paul seems to be addressing two groups, the Gentile Christians and the Jewish Christians. These perplexing issues probably threatened to divide the church. Of course, it was not just in Rome that these problems arose, and Paul has to address the same issues with almost all the Christian churches. The problem is understandable. The Jews, even those who now believed that Jesus was the Messiah, had been instructed since childhood to keep the Torah. Many of them believed that one could not be a child of Abraham, a Covenant member, unless one was circumcised, if male, and kept the Torah faithfully. They believed they could just add to the Torah the belief that Jesus is the Messiah.

Paul endeavours to show both groups that the Torah was indeed good and God-given, but that it had now been fulfilled in Christ for us. Both groups needed to see the big picture of God's plan for humanity, and the strange purpose of the Jews and Torah in that plan."

"I don't see it either, Reverend Thomas. What was the point, and how has it been fulfilled?" Melvyn asked.

"Please call me Robert," Reverend Thomas suggested. "The picture, rather facile and incomplete I admit, I use to help people understand how the Torah has been fulfilled is to think of last week's TV Times. There was nothing wrong with last week's TV Times. It was good and accurate and served its purpose, but it has been fulfilled and is no longer of use."

"That makes sense, Robert. Thanks! I've taken my Bible along. Maybe we could skim through Romans and you can show me the flow of the reasoning. I can take notes to help me in my personal reading later, and you can call me Melvyn"

"I'd be delighted, Melvyn," Robert beamed.

They both opened their Bibles to the Book of Romans, and Robert summarized the topic of each chapter while Melvyn scribbled away furiously.

"The introduction in chapter one you will have understood. Then from verse eighteen Paul catalogues the dehumanizing downward spiral of humanity, back into darkness and death, from the time sin entered the world onwards. Ominously God lets humans have their way. The Jews in Rome will no doubt think Paul is talking to their Gentile brothers and sisters, at this point.

In chapter two he addresses those (Jews, of course) who assume they are not part of this world of wickedness, and look down on Gentile sinners and their vile practices. However he accuses both Jews and Gentiles of horrendous wickedness."

"This is one of the things I don't get," Melvyn interrupted. "It seems to me that Paul is preaching a salvation through good works here, and not a 'right standing before God by trusting him,' that he mentions in chapter one."

"Yes, I see," Robert replied. "Paul is not contradicting himself. He is talking in chapter one of being assured in advance of the verdict of 'not guilty' for our sins on the Day of Judgement, through faith in Christ, which he will explain fully later in the book. In chapter two he is also talking of the Day of Judgment, but as a day when all our sins will be exposed and all wrongs will have to be acknowledged, since God has promised to right all wrongs that occur in this life. In other words, while all evil behaviour will be condemned, the final verdict for all who have faith in the Messiah is exoneration, since the Messiah took the verdict 'guilty' on himself to gift believers the verdict 'not guilty'. That is what we in the trade call 'justification by faith'. The guilty are declared not morally innocent, which of course we are not, but 'not guilty' and therefore not punishable. Of course, they are also gifted through union with Messiah, his righteous human status gained through his life of perfect obedience to the Father."

"Now I see," Melvyn said. "Our behaviour has to be exposed for what it is and we have to face those we have wronged. God's justice and judgment will be completely fair and impartial and will be seen to be so. I think deep down every human being longs for that kind of justice. God would not be a good God if he did not make sure every wrong is righted, and every sordid deed is exposed. Still that is a very scary prospect."

"Indeed you are right. We don't want to face the truth about ourselves, or the consequences of our behaviour when we are in the wrong, but we have to. However at the same time as he shows us our sins, known and unknown, he will also show us how he has already taken care of things, making all things new and right. We will be gratefully amazed at the creative genius of our merciful God. He can turn horrible events around and bring good out of even horrendous evil. It will be a just putting right, but without condemnation since Christ has already suffered in our place.

The second half of chapter two comes down hard on any Jews who believe only they have a special relationship with God. Jews may try to justify this belief on the grounds that God made a Covenant with them and gave them the Torah, which is the embodiment of knowledge and truth, and because he gave them a sign of the Covenant, circumcision. Paul tells them that these things have no value to Jews who break the Torah, and that circumcision of the heart, by the Spirit, is the only circumcision that really counts before God. Outward circumcision was only a sign that pointed to the reality, a reality now fulfilled in the cutting or writing of the Law on believers' hearts.

By chapter three the Gentile Christians might be feeling quite smug, even maybe asking themselves what possible advantage there might be in being a Jew. Paul reminds them that the Jews were given the Scriptures, and that in them God promises to be faithful to his Covenant with Abraham, and to bless the whole world through his progeny. Though the physical children of Abraham had not been faithful to the Covenant, God's promise to be faithful to the Covenant and to bless all the nations of the world through Abraham's children, has never been revoked. The chapter then goes on to conclude the obvious, that having the Law but not keeping it does not make a person a child of Abraham. He shows how Jews and Gentiles alike are guilty of sin.

The story does not end there, and the end of the chapter is a glorious reiteration of the Gospel. As foretold in the Old Testament Scriptures, God in faithfulness to his Covenant steps in, and through the one and only faithful child of Abraham, Jesus the Messiah, dies for, redeems, and justifies Jews and Gentiles alike. All Jews and Gentiles alike are sinners, and all alike are declared to be in the right by faith in the faith of the faithful one, Jesus Christ. There is no room for boasting or pride of any kind, because God is God of Jews and Gentiles alike, and his plan is for the whole of his creation. The question then arises, 'might Gentiles Christians be correct to assume that faith nullifies the Torah?' Paul strongly rejects any such conclusion saying that on the contrary faith upholds the Torah."

"This is very confusing!" Melvyn exclaims. "We seem to be going round in circles."

"Patience!" Robert laughed. "This is indeed dense but well worth unpacking. Chapter four goes on to explain this conclusion. The Jews might now think that Paul has come round again to advocating the keeping of Torah, but Paul shows how Abraham's faith in believing God's promises, long before Torah had been given to Moses, was what put him in a right relationship with God. Thus Abraham is the father of all who believe and are not circumcised, and all who believe and are circumcised, because they are walking in the footsteps of Abraham, who had faith both before and after his circumcision. Jews and Gentiles alike, who believe that Christ died for the sins of humanity and was resurrected and ascended for the justification of humanity, are accepted on the basis of that trust in Christ. They are all true children of Abraham, children of the Covenant."

"It all seems to fit into place. It really helps to understand that Paul is addressing two factions with different takes on God's plan, and that both are deficient in their understanding. This is great stuff and really very helpful, Robert," Melvyn said while still jotting down notes.

"I think so too," Robert admitted. "Now going on to chapter five we find more of the historical background that explains the Gospel. Paul recalls for them that there are two men who represent humanity with quite different outcomes. Adam, the first man, represents all humanity. He sinned which brought horrendous consequences into the world. From that time forward every human was born with a propensity to sin. Only Christ had the power, through the Holy Spirit's anointing, to resist this evil inclination. This was not easy for him, and he suffered greatly from being tempted, we discover in the Book of Hebrews. He too assumed fallen flesh and was subject, like us, to the temptations and attacks of the Evil One.

Christ has a right to represent humanity because he created and sustains us and because he became incarnate. In Christ we can be recreated. The first Adam represented us almost accidently as he was the first man and everyone else, including Eve, came from his body. He caused the Fall of humanity. The outcome of the representation of the last Adam far outshines that of the first Adam, and the gift he bestows on humankind is, in its sheer grace and magnitude, beyond our wildest dreams. He brought the free gift of justification and resurrection life to those dead in trespasses and sin:

'Just as one person did it wrong and got us in all this trouble with sin and death, another person got it right and got us out of it. But more than just getting us out of trouble, he got us into life! One man said no to God and put many people in the wrong; one man said yes to God and put many in the right.'

Paul adds that Torah was given to define sin and thus cause sin to be shown up in the full extent of its horror. Before the Torah was given nobody could be accused of breaking the Law, since they were ignorant of its commands.

Chapter six examines union with Christ. Christ not only represents his people but he is also united to them. That's what it means to be, 'in Christ'. What is true of him is true of us since we are, 'in Christ'. The initiation rite of Christian baptism is a sign of our dying and rising again with Christ. United to him in his death, his people are crucified and die to sin, and united to him in his resurrection, his people are raised to new life in him. Because of this we are no longer slaves to sin and no longer under the condemnation of Torah, the Law. We now live under grace in union with Christ through his Spirit. Once humanity was represented by Adam, and in him they came under the degenerating power of sin, which always leads to death. That power over us came to an end when Christ caught us up and brought us down with him, into his death, and through death on to his resurrection. Now we are represented by Christ alone.

Chapter seven explains how we died to the condemnation of the Torah through the body of Christ, so that we can now live to Christ through the Spirit. The next part of the chapter uses a literary form common in Paul's time, to give a history of the experience of living under the Torah. Paul himself is a Jew and he identifies with the history of his people by using the first person 'I'. He cannot use the "we" more common to us, as what he has to say about living under the Torah is not true of the Gentile Christians, but only of the Jewish Christians, and he is speaking to both. What he says is not true of him personally but is merely the collective truth of most people living under Torah. We know this, because he says elsewhere that he was a blameless keeper of Torah, making use of Torah's pictorial provisions for dealing with sin. He uses the same literary form in the letter to the Galatians in chapter two from verse eighteen when he is talking not of himself, but of a hypothetical situation where one seeks to go back to living under the restrictions of Torah.

In this chapter of Romans he shows how Torah defines sin, and how that makes the Jews doubly guilty, piling up their sin since they knew it was sin. Try as they might to keep Torah, they found the power of evil too great to resist. They had to acknowledge that the Torah was good, but that they were powerless to keep it. They, like the rest of humanity, were children of the first Adam, and as such part of the problem of sin in the world. They were helpless slaves of sin and complete failures in their calling to be the light of the world to the Gentiles. This piled up sin was concentrated on those who were given the Law, until it assumed its full extent in that most heinous of sins, the crucifying of the Messiah. Yet sin could only be dealt a death blow by the death of the Messiah. Paul has in mind the picture of the two goats on the Day of Atonement. One of the goats, the scapegoat, pictured the sins of all the Israelites piled on its head through the hands of the high priest, to be carried away into the wilderness. The other goat was put to death and its blood, the symbol of its forfeited life, was used to picture Christ's atonement for sin.

Chapter eight is a veritable hymn of praise to God for his rescue plan to save us from the verdict of death predicted in Eden, as the consequence of sin. Not only are believers freed from death, by the death of sin and the death of death in Christ, but they are given the Holy Spirit to live in them to help them to lead holy lives. They are being renewed after the image of Christ, and he shares his mind with them. Believers are given the power to forsake sin and embrace their status as adopted children of God. They, and all creation, long for and pray for the day when their full resurrection life will be realized. Meanwhile, in spite of weakness, suffering, and even death, nothing can separate us from the love of God in Christ Jesus, our Lord.

In chapter nine, Paul laments the fact that so few of his fellow Jews have recognized their Messiah. Jews were indeed elected, or chosen, by God to bring light to the world, and to them belonged the blessing of adoption, Covenants, Torah, worship, patriarchs, promises and even the incarnation of the Messiah. Yet they failed utterly in their mission to the world. God had elected Abraham from among his peers, then Isaac from Abraham's children, then Jacob over his twin Esau, then Israel from all the nations of the earth, to teach them the purposes of God to rescue his world from sin, death, and decay. The one man, then one family, then one nation was elected to bless the many nations but they needed themselves to be rescued. However, the good news is that those who believe, both Jews and Gentiles together, are the true children of Abraham. No longer are the natural progeny of Abraham, who do not walk in the faith of Abraham, to be called his children. They are only his children ethnically. Believers are the true children of Abraham, and they are elected in Christ for sharing Christ's light to the world, to bring others to faith in Christ also. They are, like the Jews before them, chosen not to hoard their own blessing but to share their blessing with the world.

In chapter ten Paul continues his lament for his fellow countrymen who do not believe. He understands their zeal, and their mistaken endeavour to seek life through keeping the Torah, as he himself had done at one time. Again he reiterates that believing Jews and Gentiles together make up the people of God.

Chapter eleven again addresses those who think God may have rejected Jews and now only offers salvation to Gentiles. Paul reminds them that he himself is a Jew, and that there may be more believing Jews in the world than one may think. Elijah, after all, thought he was the only believer left alive in Israel, only to be told that far from being alone, God had kept thousands of other believers alive.

Still Paul admits Israel has to a large extent rejected the Messiah. The Gospel is now being proclaimed and believed by Gentiles. Paul expresses a hope that this may eventually cause more of Paul's fellow Jews to become jealous and become believers themselves. Then Paul again counterbalances the sad state of the unbelieving Jews, with warnings to Gentile Christians not to look down on Jews, but to remember the blessings they now enjoy came to them via Israel. Israel may indeed be like branches broken off an olive tree to allow the grafting in of wild olive branches, the Gentiles, into the olive tree, but God can even more easily graft Jewish converts back into their native olive tree. Paul's heart bleeds for his fellow countrymen whose hearts have been so hardened against their Messiah, but he rejoices in the new children of Israel now made up of believing Jews plus believing Gentiles.

Chapter twelve urges all the believers together to live in a way that pleases God, by being witnesses to the world that they belong to a different way of thinking. They are also all to use their gifts to build up the church of Christ by serving one another, and encouraging each other in the faith.

Chapter thirteen encourages believers to live at peace with society and to respect the governing authorities, as some governing authority is preferable to none at all and complete lawlessness. God has appointed governments for the good of society, and Christians should be on the side of justice, and as far as possible obedient to the laws of society, including the paying of taxes, and giving respect to those in authority.

Chapters fourteen and fifteen are self-explanatory, while chapter sixteen urges that Phoebe, the minister from Cenchrea, who is to deliver Paul's letter to the Roman churches, be welcomed warmly by the Roman churches. Paul asks that she be given the respect and help she may need from the Roman churches to complete her task, which suggests she may have been expected to read and answer questions on its content. He greets by name many of the leading believers who are house church leaders, in Rome."

Melvyn had been busy taking copious notes. "Thanks, Robert, I feel this will be a great help when I get back to reading Romans. It is just the help I need."

Robert gave him his card and asked him to call if he needed further help.

Chapter Sixteen

The Reeds' Friends

The weather continued mild for the next few weeks and Melvyn spent more time outside. He walked further each day and he began to feel considerably stronger. He exchanged his walking frame for a walking stick, and made it down the nearby path to the shore, several times.

He continued to read the Bible. Robert's notes were of immense help to him. Romans made sense and he read the book several times. He went on to read Galatians, and found many of the same themes being addressed there. Again the problem in Galatia centred on the place of the Torah and circumcision, and who was and who was not, a true child of Abraham, a child of the Covenant. Certain Jews were trying to insist that all converts to Christianity should keep the Torah, be circumcised if male, keep the dietary laws, the holy days, and eat at the same table only with people who had in effect become Jews. Great pressure was being exerted on the new church, and even mature Christians such as Barnabas and the great apostle Peter, began to waiver when they were challenged over eating at the same table as Gentile believers. Paul was having none of it and he rebuked Peter for his double standard, and betrayal of the truth of the status of the Galatians believers as true Covenant members with believing Jews, even if they were not circumcised.

Paul was writing to show them that the Torah was fulfilled in the Messiah, and that Messiah alone of all humanity, had been able to live a sinless life in total obedience and loving fellowship with his Father, in the Spirit. He wrote that the Torah had been like a babysitter, attempting to keep Jews from the worst excesses of sin, helping them grow up, and pointing them to Christ. The Galatians and all believers were now free from the constraints of the Torah. They were under grace and the Spirit, and they were not to enslave themselves again under the Torah, or Christ would be of no benefit to them. Torah had done its job and had no more authority over them. In Christ they had outgrown the baby sitter, and were ready to become mature grown-ups in the Spirit. New family members now had to live by the law of love, the law now written on their hearts, as promised in the prophets, under the guidance of the Holy Spirit.

Melvyn went on to study Corinthians where Paul had to chide the believers for their worldly thinking, as they boasted of belonging to various teachers and different factions, as if they had become disciples of different philosophers, rather than members in the family of Christ. They were proud of their spiritual gifts and vied with one another to show them off in the congregations, rather than using them in love, to build up the church.

Corinth was a particularly heathen city with numerous gods, temples, and pagan customs and rituals, including male and female cult prostitution. Immorality was rife and the population prided themselves on their liberal thinking, and their undoubted abilities in rhetoric and philosophy. Many of the things held in high regard by the surrounding culture, Paul warned, were at odds with the teachings of Christ, and the values of his kingdom. Immorality of a very noxious nature had even entered the church with impunity, as the members thought they were "free" from the constraints of morality. Paul had to rebuke them severely, but his second letter to them commends their repentance, and extends his desire that the offending party be re-instated into the grace of the church, if he had turned his back on his previous behaviour.

In the letters to the Thessalonians, Paul wrote to the young church about how thrilled he was by their joyful acceptance of the Gospel, and their perseverance in spite of persecution. This was all the more remarkable since this was a church of former Gentile pagans, with no Jewish background. He touched on the problem caused by certain believers sponging off others, and misusing the common purse. He found them shaky in their doctrines about the return of Christ, and gave them further instruction on this matter. In every New Testament book Melvyn found rich depths of foundational teachings that brought the memory of Immanuel's love and reality close to him. He began to love Immanuel and revel in his closeness.

The book of Ephesians became a favourite of Melvyn's, with its panorama of the eternal plan of the Trinity to include humanity in its circle of love, through adoption.

Melvyn telephoned Robert frequently to discuss his discoveries, and to seek guidance on which books to read and in which order. Robert was thrilled with Melvyn's progress, and his perseverance in getting to grips with the teachings of the Bible. He did not question Melvyn about his faith but left the Holy Spirit to guide Melvyn to faith in the Messiah. Robert had no doubt that a wonderful transformation was taking place in Melvyn's heart. His hunger to understand, and his delight in finding God to be so loving, so kind, so rational, and so determined to rescue his creation was evidence enough for Robert.

Melvyn himself was aware of the transformation that had taken place in his thinking. He was excited at the realization that the Holy Spirit was right there by him, opening up the meaning of the Bible to him, and showing him more and more of Immanuel. At times he was so caught up in the joy of the revelation, that he just let the Bible drop, closed his eyes and breathed in the exquisite wonder of it all. He had read the Bible as a child and young teenager, but this was quite different. At that time he read the history, the stories, the theology and the words of the Bible, and they were to him as the words of other books. Now when he read the same words in the Bible they came to life and he encountered the Living Word.

He still had not talked to Angelina. He decided he would talk to Robert openly about his new found faith next time he was at the hospital. He must ask him for advice on how best to approach the subject with Angelina.

Angelina spent as little time as possible with Melvyn. They no longer liked each other for she had long since sensed his hostility, disapproval, and disappointment in her. He was indeed disappointed in their marriage. They had been unwise in not leaving enough time to get to know each other properly, before rushing into marriage. She was not the person he had thought he was marrying. They had tried to be civil to each other, but found it more and more difficult as time went by. They often hurt each other with cruel words and looks. Each was determined to live for the time being with the disappointment, but to get their strokes elsewhere.

Angelina did not like sick people, and Melvyn's illness was bordering on the last straw for her. She had no plans for sacrificing what remained of her life to looking after a frail old man she did not even like. Though they usually ate dinner together they had little to talk about, and she chose to go out afterwards or retire to her room complaining of tiredness. There she watched television or read, and often Melvyn did not see her until after work the following day. She never asked how he was and he never volunteered to tell her, unless he had a significant milestone such as being able to walk to the seashore, or a hospital appointment, to report.

An occasional friend came round in the evening, but Angelina discouraged this. If someone phoned up asking to visit, Melvyn often heard Angelina making excuses for him: Melvyn was too weak or not well enough to receive visitors, or she was exhausted from looking after him, and would rather not have visitors just yet. Melvyn did not really care. He was still very easily fatigued and the banter of visitors, intent on cheering him up, was tedious. The majority of their mutual friends were from the university where Melvyn had taught. He was now retired and had started writing a book which, of course, had not been touched since his operation. He had to admit to himself that he had, in any case, lost interest in the subject of his research and writing.

Nowadays he preferred his own company, as he had so much to think about, and so many new ideas to work out. He had no clue how to communicate his new found faith and doubts to Angelina. Apart from Robert, he had only one Christian friend who might be able to help him. He knew Angelina liked her, although she was a Christian. Angelina liked to believe this showed her liberality, and tolerance towards those of different philosophical persuasions.

Ellen was a molecular geneticist, who worked at the research facility of the local university, and who sometimes gave lectures around the country. They had first met her when she and a fellow scientist were holding a much publicized public debate on the case, or otherwise, for intelligent design being behind life on earth. Ellen was a fine debater, razor sharp and witty, but gracious in both victory and defeat. Her opponent that night was Fredrick Hamilton, a well-known atheist in the same field, and a friend of Ellen's but from a different university. He had just written a book claiming science had, or would soon have, all the answers to the origins and proliferation of life on earth. He claimed in his book there really was no need for any form of intelligent design theory to explain the origins of life, and the subsequent evolution of the species. He was especially scathing in dismissing what he called the primitive superstitious belief in a divine creator, such as he knew his opponent was about to advocate, or a 'god of the gaps'.

Melvyn did not remember much of what Fredrick Hamilton said that night. He was an interesting and charismatic speaker who held everyone's attention. It all sounded very reasoned and reasonable to Melvyn, and pretty much aligned itself with what he already believed, which was that there was no god and no need to believe in a god. Primitive people made up gods, to give themselves some handle on the unpredictability of life. They could try to appease the gods and in so doing have some say in their own prosperity and security. Religion had done society little good and much evil, keeping people, even today, shackled in superstition and lies. Wars were often fought in the name of some religion or other and great suffering had been inflicted on innocent populations, for no good reason. Indeed reasonable people must rid themselves and their children of stupid false hopes in a hereafter, and concentrate on making life on earth in the here and now better for everyone. Our only hope is in ourselves, and the application of science is the discipline that has made most advances for the good of humankind in medicine, technology, and other fields of study. Most of the audience were acknowledged atheists, and loud applause filled the auditorium at the close of Fredrick Hamilton's speech.

Polite clapping greeted Ellen as she rose to give her presentation. She began by denying that any conflict existed between science and Christianity. She herself was a Christian and a scientist. The Bible claims that God created everything but that does not preclude the study of the universe and every created thing in it. It does not claim to be a science manual with the answer to the way everything works. It is a book that chronicles the relationship between the Creator, his creatures, and his creation, and his good plans for that creation. Science that studies created matter and applies its findings for the good of humanity is not to be condemned as an enemy of Christianity. It is not a case that the more science reveals how things work, the less Christianity matters. Science and Christianity are dealing with different spheres of reality that are not in opposition. Only when some scientists claim that there is no Creator, and that science can prove this, do the two come into conflict. Such claims must be acknowledged for what they are – theories. Theories are simply hunches that await verifiable data to prove or disprove their validity. No theory can or ever will disprove the existence of a Creator God. Claiming that science has already proved this, and that everyone should embrace atheism, is simply not science.

As for the death and destruction caused by religious fanatics, she acknowledged the truth of this. Any coercion of religious or other beliefs was evil, and had no warrant in true Christianity. Yet atheism was not immune from the same charge of deadly intolerance. One only had to look at the twin atheistic totalitarian systems, tried out in Russia and China, to realize something of the extent of the torture and killings that took place under them in the last century.

She saw her job that evening as shedding light on the weakness and improbability of the position that the universe, and everything and everyone in it, is the product of random events. She continued by ceding to some of the claims of evolution. After all, she explained, we can see that evolution has taken place in dogs and other species, and in many plants. No problem arises from believing that evolution sometimes takes place, though questions of changeover of organs and organ systems have by no means been proved or even explained. For instance if one accepts a common ancestor for all living animals, a very great problem arises in explaining how cold blooded reptiles that produce eggs that hatch outside the body into fully functioning baby reptiles, could develop into a new species of warm blooded mammals that have a uterus, placenta and mammary glands, in addition to a completely different breathing system. For a new species to develop, a co-ordinated set of changed systems such as the breathing and circulatory systems must come into place, and must immediately work together perfectly, in order for the animal to live and survive for even a few minutes. Then for this new species to survive into the next generation, the new systems must have at least one male and one female, or some form of reproduction in place, that would propagate the species. Still heaven forbid, that she should advocate a divine creator on the basis of the "gaps".

However she went on to spell out how a much greater problem arises when people fail to realize that for evolution to take place at all, life must already be present. Without life there is not, and never can be, any form of evolution. Any type of artificially produced life depends on bits and pieces from already existing life. Thus she was not going to spend time arguing for or against the niceties of evolution, as evolution does not explain the origins of life.

Instead she asked the audience to imagine a co-worker receiving an email from a computer. The email had crossed the Atlantic, transmitting information to a device a continent away, and yet making perfect sense to the recipient who then acted on it. Communication had taken place from one computer machine to another and from the email sender to the email recipient. Surely all are agreed that such communication requires intelligent design, not only in the making of the machines but also in the operation of sending and receiving rational messages that can be acted upon. All computers are designed and programmed by human beings using only two numbers, zero and one. It would surely stretch any imagination to believe that these things could happen apart from intelligent design.

Ellen went on to explain in layman's terms the more complicated by far communication that takes place in the living molecules of all organisms, from tiny creatures to human beings. This communication takes place using only four letters for their initial activity and subsequent maintenance, which produce just the right cells for different blood, bone, tissue, brain, and other cells, at just the right stage of development and in just the right place, to form a body that sees, hears, moves, breathes, thinks, speaks, feels, eats, sleeps, reasons, reproduces, and a myriad other things, such as communicating with others and making machines that communicate information that can be accessed simultaneously by millions of computers, in millions of homes and offices, across the world. A mind is needed to design the giving and receiving of information, even of the simplest most primitive kind. A very intelligent mind indeed is required to create the life of even one tiny creature, far less that of a human being and the myriad species on earth, developed with or without the aid of evolution.

She also went on to explain that although DNA has been unravelled and studied and its workings observed, the mind that programmed its four letters to do what they do, remains a mystery to all atheist scientists. These workings are as complex, each part doing its job, as a modern day city with its many workers with their many tasks, all contributing to the smooth running of the whole. Orders are given and received and laws are in place that are obeyed, but who starts the process and keeps it going, no atheist scientist has ever been able to explain. Ellen went on to ask her opponent that night if this were not so.

Fredrick had to admit he had no definitive answer, but he had no intention of believing in a god of the unexplained. Though he still felt confident life had begun on earth by accident, no one could say exactly how. He felt sure that sometime a better answer could be found and verified. It was just unreasonable to believe otherwise. An uncomfortable rustle ran through the audience as this was not the reply they expected.

Laughter broke out when Ellen further went on to ask whether Fredrick could really expect her to put any rational faith in his intelligence, which after all he claimed was the random product of a non-intelligent haphazard selection process.

Ellen said she could only call his belief a faith. She then acknowledged her own faith. She realised that even if she could convince everybody in the audience that intelligent design was behind life, it would not prove the existence of the triune God of love she believed in. Intelligent design could only prove the existence of one or more intelligent minds, not the existence of a personal God. However like the mind of the triune God, such a mind could have no beginning; it must have had life in itself and must have been able to design and impart life.

It could not be a created life. It had to be outside creation to create another life as we know it.

Ellen admitted that she could no more prove the existence of God than she could prove to a sceptical audience the existence of her loving husband at home. She did have such a husband. Some of the audience knew him, and she did have a picture of him in her wallet, but if someone chose to disbelieve her what could she do? They could tell her they did not believe her, that he was a figment of her imagination and that the picture in her wallet could be of any man. In such a case all she could say was that she knew she did have such a husband at home, whether or not they believed her. In much the same way she knew God as a separate being. She could often feel his presence through the Holy Spirit when she prayed, when she read Scripture, when she worshipped with other believers, and in her day to day activities. She had the written testimony of others who had seen him after his resurrection. She had a picture of sorts of him from the Bible, related by people who knew him and were contemporaries of his, during his life on earth. It told of the loving character and actions of Jesus Christ, who is the incarnation of the living God. He came to earth to reveal to humans what God is really like, and to put this messed up world to rights. When the Gospel about him is preached, faith is awakened in hearts like hers and the mysteries of science, among other things, start to unfold.

That does not preclude the further study of the mysteries of how cells work, but only the answer to the vexed question of the origins of how such intricate systems were first put into motion. When a tiny glimpse of the awesome glory of this intelligence, this creativity, this power and this love shines through in the person of Jesus Christ, all one can do is fall to one's knees, cover one's face, and worship him.

An embarrassed hush fell over the audience followed by muted, polite applause. Melvyn looked at Angelina, but like himself and many in the audience, the explanation of the communication between molecules and the consequent significance of this, fell on uncomprehending ears. Angelina stifled a yawn behind her long false finger nails, and Melvyn thought she had probably been thinking of something else while the debate was going on.

However after the debate, they and some other guests were invited for refreshments to a colleague's house. Ellen was there as guest of honour, and her warm personality, sense of humour, and genuine friendliness touched everyone. Fredrick Hamilton stopped in briefly and they sparred good-humouredly.

"Ellen, you're never going to get an intelligent audience like this to give up their common sense to believe in your God," Fredrick quipped.

"You mean I should trust the by-product of a by-chance, non-intelligently programmed set of grey cells?" Ellen quipped back.

Fredrick laughed and hugged Ellen. He said bye to everyone as he had to rush off to catch a plane.

Melvyn was surprised at how much Angelina enjoyed Ellen's company. As Melvyn well knew, Angelina often made a good impression when she first met someone. She had a prodigious memory, read several weekly magazines, especially the editorials, and she was able to pass off the opinions expressed in them as her own, and may even have believed they were her own opinions. Thus to many people she seemed very well informed, and at the same time she gave the impression of being very intelligent. Those who got to know her better came to realize that her reasoning powers were actually rather weak, and only her ability to quote others was impressive.

Ellen gave Angelina the opportunity to talk extensively, listening to her quietly as she talked on various subjects. Angelina then asked Ellen if she was familiar with the recent scientific break-through at the CERN Super Collider in Geneva.

Ellen explained that she was a molecular geneticist and not a particle physicist. She said she had only a very vague notion of what went on in the seventeen mile circular tunnel five hundred feet below the ground. One of her friends working at the Large Hadron Collider had tried to explain the science involved to her, but she did not fully understand what went on there. Her friend had explained that apparently there are two types of particles, hadrons which have internal structure and leptons which have no structure. Somehow one type of hadron, protons, are made to accelerate at extremely high speeds and then collide with each other in the hope of being able to find clues as to the fundamental makeup of matter, and even the explanation for the dark holes and dark energy in the universe. Ellen said she was impressed that it took such a huge collider and so many years of research, to study such small particles of creation. She found the whole idea awesome, and it made her marvel at the mind of God, but she did not understand the science involved.

As usual, Angelina recapped what she had read in various magazines and periodicals. She said she was interested in the "god particle" which she believed was the same as the "Higgs boson" particle, named after the

Scotsman, Peter Higgs, who first theorized that there is a field that interacts with particles to give them mass. She was also interested to read of new research into matter and anti-matter, with possible imbalances that may have allowed matter to have been formed in the first place, and the experiments going on to test these theories using neutrinos. Ellen smiled and confessed her almost total ignorance, but no doubt what Angelina had read was accurate. Angelina was flattered by Ellen's attention and asked her out to lunch. The two agreed to meet for lunch the following week. Angelina's office, where she worked as a paralegal, was not far from the university where Ellen worked.

Over the following months when Ellen was not afield, the two met every few weeks for lunch. When Ellen asked Angelina and Melvyn to dinner they met Ellen's husband, James, who was a retired doctor. All their children were grown up and the two couples began to go out together every month or two for dinner, or to a play, or concert. They continued to enjoy each other's company until Melvyn's illness.

Since his operation, Melvyn had seen very little of Ellen and James. They had visited him in hospital but Melvyn had been much too ill to pay much attention to them. Since then, Melvyn felt sure Angelina had discouraged them from coming to see him at home.

Melvyn made up his mind to ask Angelina to have them over to the house for lunch one weekend. Angelina was no cook, but she could put together a very nice lunch using prepared foods from the local delicatessen. He himself could make a sandwich but otherwise was a total flop in the kitchen. Meanwhile he must ask Robert for his advice on how to tell Angelina about his new found faith.

Chapter Seventeen

Angelina's Decision

Melvyn telephoned Robert the following day but was unable to reach him. He left a message asking Robert to call him back as he had something important to tell him, and ask him. Robert called back while he and Angelina were eating dinner. As he was being overheard he could not talk openly to Robert, but he did manage to arrange a lunch time meeting for later that week, at the hospital. Angelina raised her eyebrows but said nothing.

"I'm feeling a lot stronger, Angelina," he explained. "I think I should make an effort to get out among people again. In fact, I was thinking only yesterday, that it would be nice to ask Ellen and James to lunch sometime soon. If the weather keeps warm we could have salads and stuff from the deli, on the terrace. What do you think?"

"Fine, you arrange it with them and I'll pick up the food," Angelina agreed.

Melvyn heaved an inward sigh of relief but he still worried about how it would all turn out. He could see Angelina was suspicious about his meeting with the hospital chaplain, and she might well be suspicious about an invitation to Ellen and James as well.

His lunch meeting with Robert was wonderful. Robert was ecstatic and hugged Melvyn when he told him he had come to believe in the reality of God as Father, Son, and Spirit, and that he now felt included in their amazing circle of love. Melvyn told him that his big worry now was how to share this news with Angelina, without further alienating her. Melvyn told Robert their relationship was not good, and he felt no love for her. He asked how he should go about telling her.

"That's a tough one, Melvyn. I'll certainly pray for you but I have no words of wisdom as to how you should tell Angelina. With no love for her in your heart, I'm afraid this will be just another issue that will drive you further apart. All love comes from God, and you are going to have to ask Christ to put his love for Angelina, into your heart. You are going to have to pray to see Angelina as Christ sees her."

"How can I love her when I don't love her? I don't even like her far less love her," Melvyn moaned.

"Apart from praying for her and yourself, you can make a start by being considerate towards her, even if you don't like her. You can do things for her that you think she might like. You can talk respectfully to her and even praise her whenever you can. You can buy her little presents, and go with her to events and places that interest her. You can do the sort of things you did when you were first in love. However if she does decide to leave you, you will have to let her go without rancour. The Bible does talk of letting an unbelieving spouse be the one to decide whether or not to end the marriage.

If Angelina decides to stay with you, you will have to learn to love her again. That may not be in the same way as you once did, but it must be sacrificially and unconditionally, as you promised in your wedding vows. For the moment, just take it one step at a time, and ask for the Spirit to help you to love Angelina with Christ's love."

"I feel very guilty because I don't love her," Melvyn admitted. "Christ loves me even although I am a mess."

"Yes, he does," Robert agreed, "and he loves Angelina too. We must pray together that he shares his love for Angelina with you."

"I don't want to love her. I don't want to share in Christ's love for Angelina. I don't want to put the effort into something that bores me, and makes no sense to me. I'm despicable I know."

"Then maybe we have to go deeper down, and pray that Christ will give you the desire to share in his love for Angelina. Do you think you could do that?"

"I'll try. I don't think I can live with myself if I don't."

Robert prayed with Melvyn, and then he had to leave for his next appointment. They hugged and smiled a sad goodbye, since both of them felt the burden of Melvyn's lack of love for Angelina weighing them down. Melvyn sat on at the table thinking of what he would say to Angelina. Still undecided he at last got up, and went to a nearby florist shop. There he bought Angelina a bunch of sweet peas, her favourite flowers, before taking a taxi home.

The decision was taken out of his hands before he had a chance to tell Angelina of his new found faith. He found a note on the table telling him that since he was better, she was moving out. She would be coming back to pick up her things over the next few days, and then he would be hearing from her lawyer. She said she was sorry their marriage turned out to be such a mistake for both of them, but it was silly to keep up the pretence any longer.

Melvyn did not know whether to laugh or cry. Relief and shame for feeling relief, vied with guilt for the shallowness of his past love for Angelina, and his present lack of love for her. He sat down, head in hands, and tried to pray. Darkness slowly fell but still he could not find the words to talk to the God who loved him so much, in spite of his own lack of love. In the end he rose, switched on the light and sighed, "God forgive me. I don't even know what to say to you. I want to be like you and to love like your Son. Please help me…"

It was then the Spirit brought the words from the Bible into his mind: "God's Spirit is right alongside helping us along. If we don't know how or what to pray, it doesn't matter. He does our praying in and for us, making prayer out of our wordless sighs, our aching groans."

"Thank-you, Spirit. Thank-you, Spirit for praying for me even when I cannot pray for myself. Thank-you, Spirit for bringing me the comfort of your words. Please, Spirit, show Angelina the Way. Show her the Truth and the reality of your love for her. She is gone from me but she is not gone from you. Please help her, Lord, as you have helped me. Please, Lord."

Melvyn sat up most of the night wordlessly mulling over things. At last he reached for his Bible and found the words that had comforted him so much. He read them again.

"I have so much to learn," he thought. "I have to change such a lot, if ever I am going to be fit to live in Immanuel's kingdom."

He undressed and lay down in bed. Tears welled up in his eyes and tumbled down his cheeks. He dried them on the sheet, turned over on his side, curled into a foetal position and eventually fell into a deep sleep.

"Surprise! Surprise, Granddad! We've come to see you! Get up, it's ten o'clock!" Melvyn's grandchildren roared into his ears. "It's a lovely day, Granddad. May we go down to the shore?"

Melvyn came to slowly, "Yes, yes! Give me a minute!"

"Are you okay, Dad?" Karen asked anxiously.

"Yes, I think so. I just had a very late night," Melvyn replied. "Is Adam here?"

"Yes, I'm here! Look, why don't I take the kids down to the beach and let you have time to get up?" Adam suggested.

"Good idea, Adam. I'll go and put some coffee on and give Dad time to shower and dress. Where's Angelina?" Karen asked.

"I'll tell you over coffee," Melvyn sighed.

The children and Adam were already half way out the door. Karen made her way to the kitchen and put coffee on to perk. She noticed the sweet peas on the counter looking rather limp. Taking them out of the wrapper she found a vase and set them in water. Knowing they were Angelina's favourite flowers Karen sensed something was wrong. Her father and Angelina must have quarrelled.

The delicate perfume from the flowers, as she set them on the table, mixed with the pungent smell of the coffee. She found some mugs and milk, and began to heat the croissants she had brought. By the time Melvyn appeared, showered and shaven, though somewhat pale, the coffee was ready and a plate of hot, buttered croissants added to the good smells in the kitchen.

"That smells so good, Karen," Melvyn smiled. He had not eaten the previous evening and was really quite hungry.

"We thought we'd come down for the day and surprise you, as the weather is so wonderful and the kids love to play on the beach."

"It's very kind of you and the timing is perfect. Angelina has left me, and I don't want to be alone today," Melvyn admitted showing Karen the note Angelina had left for him. He drank some milky coffee and tucked slowly into part of a warm croissant, while Karen glanced over the note.

"I can't say I'm all that surprised, Dad. I am sorry but I'm not surprised. Angelina is not an easy person to live with, and she certainly is not one of my favourite people." They finished eating, and at Melvyn's suggestion they took their coffees into the conservatory.

"What was the final straw that decided Angelina, may I ask?"

"Well, it hasn't exactly been a barrel of laughs for her these last few months, and I suspect the final straw was her suspicion that I had become a Christian."

"You, a Christian? What? Is that true, Dad? Have you become a believer?" Karen asked in amazement. "Oh, Dad, I am so very happy for you. Have you really?"

"Believe it or not I have," Melvyn admitted.

"I can't believe it! You of all people! No wonder Angelina left you. She hates Christianity. Just because you change you can't expect her to change, but we'll have to pray for her. I'm so happy for you, Dad. This is just wonderful news. How did it happen?" Karen was laughing and crying at the same time. Melvyn was smiling and chuckling.

"Well, Karen, I've had time over the last few months to do a lot of thinking. It started with some strange, but very real dreams I had in hospital. I won't bore you with the details just now. Actually the details embarrass me, but maybe another time I'll tell you. You know I have been an atheist most of my life and was horrified when you became a Christian believer, and married a believer. I blamed your mother. She always had a sinister way of influencing you."

"Dad," Karen broke in, "you can't blame Mom for changing her beliefs, or me for being convinced by her. You rejected her because she could no longer hold to your views about God."

"There were other things ..."

"No doubt there were. There always are," Karen ceded. "Anyway, do continue!"

"Be that as it may, I started reading the Bible again to see if the things I saw in my dreams lined up with the teaching there. Horror of horrors they did, and it started making a lot of sense to me. The triune God has become very real to me. I feel Christ very near to me through his Spirit, showing me what his Father is really like. God is not at all who I imagined him to be, or what as a child I was taught he was like. The Bible is showing me someone who passionately loves humanity, and all his creation, and who will stop at nothing to put it to rights again. I had come to believe the Bible was just a book of rules and regulations, with a blood thirsty hanging-judge God, who had been invented by a primitive society. I did believe the New Testament teachings of Christ were quite reasonable, but that the events of his life must be mostly embellishments by his disciples. I scoffed at stories of miraculous healings, and of his resurrection. His claims to be divine I thought showed he must be a bit mad or deluded, in spite of his other teachings."

Tears filled Karen's eyes again. She rose and put her arms around her father.

"I can see it has been a struggle for you. Thank-you for sharing this with me! This is the most wonderful news. You don't know what this means to me."

Before Melvyn could reply a ring from the doorbell made them look out. James and Ellen were at the front door.

"Oh no, I forgot all about James and Ellen coming to lunch today. Would you let them in, darling?"

"How very nice it is to see you again! Ellen, James, do come in!" Karen said ushering them into the conservatory. "Will you have some coffee?"

"That would be lovely!" the visitors agreed and Karen went to make some fresh coffee, and to get some more mugs and some more warm croissants.

While she was gone, Melvyn explained Angelina's absence and why he was still having his first coffee of the day.

"I'm sorry Angelina has left you. It's a long time since we've been out together, but I sensed you two have been having your problems. She needs our prayers," Ellen began, "but I am thrilled beyond anything that you have become a believer, Melvyn. Welcome to the family!" She rose and hugged him.

"Melvyn, this is wonderful news!" James rose and joined in hugging Melvyn. "How on earth did it happen?"

Melvyn gave them the same short version he had given Karen. Karen brought in the coffee and they talked, laughed, and cried over Melvyn and his news. They were all very much aware of the Spirit's presence with them. A holy love had joined them and they sensed it. The day together stretched into lunch, bought from the deli, when Adam and the children returned. Melvyn then rested. Later after a trip to the grocery store, Adam and Jim cooked everyone a BBQ for dinner, before the party had to break up and they had to leave for home.

"Don't worry about your father, Karen, we'll look out for him," Ellen assured Karen.

"I know you will. That's very kind of you!" Karen replied. "Dad is doing a lot better, and I think he is going to be just fine. We'll be down next weekend again."

Melvyn laughed. "Thank-you for coming and don't worry about me. Karen bought me a heap of ready meals when she went to the grocery store, and I've got a microwave. It's not the first time I've been on my own. Anyway I'm not on my own any longer. Immanuel, our God is with me all the time!"

Chapter Eighteen

Melvyn has more Questions

During the next few months Karen and her family often made Saturday trips to check on her father. In spite of his continuing fatigue they could see that Melvyn was much better. Melvyn still did not know if he would be having further treatment. He had not been strong enough so far for any radical treatment, but there was a chance he would not need it in any case. Ellen and James kept their promise, and looked in on or phoned Melvyn almost every day. James, being retired, was the one who visited Melvyn more often. Reverend Thomas also visited and phoned Melvyn from time to time. Both men, and Ellen when she was around, enjoyed lively conversations with Melvyn, as he developed a more thorough theological understanding. The Spirit was bringing the Scriptures to life for Melvyn, and solidifying the reality of his recent experiences, as day by day he read, prayed, and meditated on his new found faith.

Melvyn shared with James his nagging dread of the fate of those who rejected their place in the circle of love, of the Triune God.

"I had this horrific dream while I was in hospital, James. People were tearing each other apart in a huge, smouldering, rubbish dump. The hate and cruelty were beyond words, and an evil presence seemed to be pacing up and down egging the fiendish mob on. What do you believe about hell, James? Does God really allow this to happen?" Melvyn asked.

"There are many theories about hell, Melvyn. The picture language Christ and the apostles used about hell is understood literally by some people, as you know. Other people understand these passages in Scripture to be speaking of hell as an annihilation, or a banishment to the dark nothingness, from which creation was called forth, in the first place. When Christ talked of people being thrown into hell fire, it was the fire that never went out and it was the worm that never died, not the people. Certainly those who were thrown into hell suffered weeping and gnashing of teeth but it could have been momentarily. The Jewish image of punishment after death, in Christ's time, was Gehenna. Gehenna was actually a huge fly and maggot- infested rubbish dump outside Jerusalem that smouldered night and day, and its master the devil was called Lord of the Flies.

One thing we can be sure of is that God is not going to have any trace of cruelty, hate, injustice, selfishness, greed, or evil in his new kingdom. Only love, kindness, goodness, purity, and right relationships can survive in his presence. Those who reject God's love and choose evil may have their fill of it. Some people believe that the fire flowing from God's throne, pictured in Daniel and Revelation, is actually a fire of mercy that keeps the wicked from approaching God. The wicked would be utterly consumed if they got near God, and this fire may be another expression of God's love, as the lesser of two evils for defiant sinners, giving them space to have a change of mind."

Melvyn thought about that and it gave him some resolution. He would have to give the problem some more thought.

"Another thing I find truly confusing, James, is the way that even believers in the Old Testament times hung on to their household gods. For instance, Rachel stole and hid the household gods of her father, although she was a believer. Why did she want to hang on to them? Also the Israelites were asked to get rid of their household gods by Joshua after they entered Canaan, which implied they possessed and worshipped them while in the desert, after coming out of Egypt. What do you think?"

James smiled. "I don't think we are much different today," he laughed. "We are Christians who love God, and yet we cling to our little gods. Some of us harbour the desire for fame, some of us harbour the desire for riches, some of us worship our place in the world, our physical appearance, our athletic prowess, our talents, our brain power, the reflected glory of our 'successful' children, spouse, friend, or the image (good word for it) that we project to the world, and a host of other secret vices. We can detect our cherished household gods when we get angry over snubs, or perceived attacks, or rubbishing, of our precious longings. We all have household gods that often take precedence over the One True God."

"Wow! I never thought of that. That's certainly something to keep aware of and throw out fast."

"The trouble I find with myself," James admitted, "is that I throw them out, and then go back to find them again. It is not usually a one-off event."

"I see!" Melvyn nodded.

"The Western world also has its mega-gods, principally Mammon. Our global economic systems depend, for the most part, on entire countries being enslaved by crippling debt through massive loans from rich countries, at such high interest rates that they can never be paid off. Third world and developing nations are often kept in abject poverty to fund our opulent life-styles," James continued.

"But what is the answer?" Melvyn asked.

"I think we could take a page out of the Old Testament at this point, and forgive debts after seven years or at least after fifty years, as in the year of Jubilee. Perhaps then poor countries could begin to stand on their own feet. Of course there are always other problems too, in getting the officials and rulers to act justly towards their own people. Corruption is always a problem in poor countries, with aid being syphoned off to inflate the purses of the powerful. In poor countries the rich get richer at the expense of the often abject poor. It happens in more developed countries too."

"Roll on the kingdom of our Lord and Saviour, Jesus Christ!" Melvyn sighed.

"Yes, yes to that!" James agreed.

With Robert, Melvyn discussed more complex points of theology, especially the different views among Christians on the nature of salvation, and the part Christ played to achieve it.

"Robert, I'm still very perplexed by the doctrine of predestination. I know you explained to me that in Roman chapter nine, which formed the core of my father's belief, Paul is talking of the election of Israel as the ones who were chosen to bring light to the world.

The one nation was elected, not to exclude the others, but to bless the others. They failed of course in this task, but God remained faithful to his Covenant promises to Abraham and to the Jewish nation. Christ then became, as God always envisioned, the Chosen One who was rejected by humans but precious to God. Christ was the true Israelite, the Elect One of God that took away the sins of the world. Christ had to fulfil and complete Israel's mission to be the light of the world to bless the world. I understand all that, but that does not seem to me to be the whole picture.

I've been looking again at chapter eight of Romans and verses twenty-nine and thirty which seems to support the position that the elect are those whom God knew beforehand would believe, and so he then predestined them. It seems in some ways fairer than the whole thing being predetermined, but it takes the initiative out of God's hands, and we're told we did not choose God but that he chose us. What do you think, Robert?" Melvyn asked.

"I think what we have to look at first is the way straightforward language can become loaded with very particular meanings. Take the word 'elect' and what does it mean in common usage – chosen? selected? Then look at the term as used in the theological circles we were both brought up in. There we find that God is said to have elected only some people, the elect, from before time to be saved; the remainder are to be passed over, but at the same time they are condemned and punished for not believing. To them I respond that in the first place the Bible never teaches that God ever chose some to be rejected; that is a position deduced from the belief that if he chose some for life, then he must have chosen the others for death, or at least left them to perish. This is a Western type reasoning but not biblical teaching. This is very important as we end up in all kinds of unbiblical knots if we go further than the Bible's teaching.

The second point is that if some are to be condemned for not believing in Christ we have to look at what that means. What is it that they do not believe? Do they believe that they are not part of the elect? If so, according to this particular understanding of the doctrine of election, they believe the truth about themselves, which is that they are not part of the elect. Are they to be condemned for believing the truth about themselves? I think not. It also cannot be for not believing that Christ died and rose and ascended for them, since according to this doctrine of election he did not.

The third point is that everywhere in the Bible it talks of us being elect, or chosen, 'in Christ'. Our Western individualism lets us down when we come to the Bible's teaching on the chosen ones. God chose the Hebrews to bring light to the Gentiles; they were the chosen ones, the elect of God. That did not mean that every individual in the chosen ones was a believer. We find numerous examples of Hebrews who rejected God. Not every natural born child of Abraham was a believer.

When it comes to the New Testament, what the Bible teaches is that God chose or elected to save humans, not angels. In Hebrews we read of the condemnation of those who trample underfoot the blood of Christ that saved them. God saved the reprobate but they reject the provision of salvation Christ achieved for them. Romans chapter five also makes the extent of salvation to humanity amply clear. All who died in the first Adam are made alive in the last Adam. If we understand this then we should have no trouble with the doctrine of election, and have no reason to accept either of the positions you outlined. God chose humanity in Christ, not specific individuals, before the foundations of the world, and we are free to accept or reject that love and mercy. First John chapter two and verse two sums this up perfectly: 'When he served as a sacrifice for our sins, he solved the problem for good – not only ours, but the whole world's.'"

Robert went on to explain that now anyone in the world can claim their sins are forgiven, through the atoning work of the Son of God. Knowing this brings the dead to life and sinners to repentance.

He further explained that believers in the Messiah now have the same mandate as ethnic Israel had to bring the Light of the World, to the world. They can only do this in union with Christ, through the Spirit. Those who believe through them are then, in turn, charged with the same mandate.

"But I still don't see that as the whole story. Romans nine says that God raised Pharaoh up for the purpose of letting the rest of the world know God's power to destroy his enemies. It also says God loved Jacob and hated Esau. What is that all about?" Melvyn queried.

"I don't pretend to understand it completely, but if you look at the stories of both these men you will find that they both defied God, and then he hardened them in their chosen states. With Esau, in spite of his knowledge and up-bringing, he chose to marry pagan wives. His progeny became increasingly degenerate, until God wiped them from the earth. Esau himself at one point repented, and married a believing wife in addition to his pagan ones, but the damage was done. In spite of this, according to Hebrews, Esau was blessed both by God and his father during his lifetime, but the consequences of his choices played out in the following generations. It is the wickedness of his descendants, the children of Esau, the Edomites, that God hated I believe. They were utterly destroyed.

As for Pharaoh, God was beyond patient with him. Time after time he flew in the face of God, and hardened his heart against all reason. In the end God gave him over to his hard heart, and the Bible goes on to record the change from Pharaoh hardening his own heart, to God hardening Pharaoh's heart. Chapter one of Romans explains much the same process happening to those who knowingly, and wilfully, reject God. God gave them over to indulge their wicked desires, and they became more and more evil, when given this so called freedom they desired."

"That certainly fits in with the Bible passages that talk of God not wanting anyone to perish, and having no pleasure in the death state of the wicked," Melvyn added. "He wants everybody to come to the knowledge that they are chosen and accepted in the Beloved. We are not then chosen in ourselves but in Christ. The gospel is all about what Christ was and is and did, and believing it changes lives. That's what changed me.

I remember there was another argument my father used to support his particular understanding of the doctrine of election. He used to argue from the pulpit that if Christ died for everyone, and some people do not come to belief, then Christ died in vain for those people.

However since Christ never does anything in vain, he could not have died for everyone."

"Yes, but if you use that dualistic argument then you can use the opposite argument, that if God desires everyone to be saved and come to a knowledge of the truth, and not everyone is saved and comes to a knowledge of the truth, then God's desire is in vain. But since God never desires anything in vain, everyone must be saved and come to a knowledge of the truth," Robert retorted.

"I never thought of that," Melvyn laughed. "Of course, neither argument is biblical or valid. They both ignore the fact that God has given us the chance to say no to his good gifts and plans for us. We are not puppets in God's hands. God wants to bring us to the point where we love him gladly and willingly."

Robert loved to explain and talk about how the Gospel must always be presented as the finished work of Christ, not as a possibility but as it is a finished deed.

"We are not saved by our faith or repentance, but by the finished work of Christ, and nothing we can do changes God's mind to make him favourable to us – not repentance, not faith, nor anything else. He is already favourable towards us. God, the Father, was in Christ reconciling the world to himself, while we were still sinners," Robert reminded Clive many times. "We were the ones that needed to be reconciled, not God, who never changes and never stopped loving us. He chose to save the world from alienation; we did not choose to repent and turn to him. Yes, we have to have our eyes opened to the truth, and believe it for it to make a difference in our lives.

It is quite legitimate, if not necessary, to ask whether a person believes the Gospel they have been told about. Christ asked one man if he believed in him, and he like many of us had to reply, 'I believe. Help me with my doubts!' Our response is more of a thank-you when we realise what God has done for us. Asking Christ into our lives, or receiving Christ into our lives, is perhaps assuming we are in charge. The triune God of Grace asks us into his life, and not the other way around. God is God, and he is not at our beck and call.

I think that knowing that everyone is included in Christ's atonement for the world makes it a lot easier for individuals to believe, that they too, are included in his saving plan for us. We're all included, and even our faith is a gift since Christ is the only one who completely believed God always, and gifts participation in that faith to us. In the same way the goodness of God leads us to repentance. Only when we see Christ in the beauty of his holiness do we see the poverty of our own righteousness, and how much he has forgiven us. Seeing that goodness, and his forgiveness of us for so much, is the only thing that will cause us to repent. Indeed in the face of such an amazing demonstration of love, the wish to be excluded from participation in the life of the triune God can only be considered totally irrational.

Some people caught in sin think that excludes them from God's mercy, but that is a low view of Christ's achievement for us, and a belief that somehow our behaviour can negate Christ's finished work. Our behaviour counts, and we do have to be changed to make us fit for the kingdom, but nothing can separate those who love him from the love of God that is in Christ Jesus, our Lord.

Still, thankfully, no inadequate presentation, or even the misunderstanding of the Gospel, cuts us off from the grace of God. The Spirit works with people where they are in their understanding, and she can begin to help them mature in spite of blind spots. I know many fine Christians from backgrounds where the Gospel is poorly taught, but who still love and serve God. We all have blind spots and if we think we haven't, that may well show we do indeed have blind spots."

Robert and Melvyn had many other interesting discussions together, encompassing topics from the beliefs of the early church fathers, to the effect of the Reformation and then the enlightenment and the age of reason, on the beliefs of the church. Melvyn was especially interested in the latter as he saw how it affected his father's view of God. Melvyn and Robert agreed that after the Reformation some scholars, starting with their own experiences and extra-biblical reasoning systems, began to forget the triune God of relationship, or at least downplay its importance. Instead of starting with the revelation of God in the being of Christ Jesus, they began to reason with their own minds, that what is good in human beings such as the attributes of justice, wisdom, holiness and truth, must be perfect in God. Thus God must be all just, all wise, all powerful, all holy, etc. etc. From there it was a short step to codifying these attributes into rational systems of theology, and confessions that had little to do with the biblical way of presenting the Gospel, and the character of the triune God. Strict adherence to these codes defined orthodoxy, and true relational godliness and the fruits of the Spirit began at times to slip into second place, in the life of the church.

Yet before there was time or space or matter God existed as Father, Son and Spirit. His essence is love and all his attributes are governed by love. It is foolish to imagine that sin changed God, and that attributes such a God's holiness can now be defined by sin. God was holy before anyone sinned and he remains holy in loving relationship. We can only be holy as he shares the fruit of the Spirit with us. It is God's fruit, not ours that he gifts to us as we are able to bear it.

Both men agreed that the Bible teaches that through Christ's character, actions, and teachings he reveals God to us. The priorities of the Bible, the love of the Father and Son in the Holy Spirit outpoured for the world, must not give way to the logic of Aristotle and a Greek way of reasoning to show us what God is like. Instead of bringing us closer to God and his loving fatherhood and awesome divinity, these flights of logic make God out to be remote, untouchable, and impersonal. His essence, love, then becomes less important than his remote and seemingly negative attributes such as holiness, implacable justice, wrath, hate, etc., instead of them being seen as part of his love.

Robert and Melvyn also discussed the other casualty of the age of reason, with the authority of the Bible being subjected to so-called higher criticism. Humans stood in judgement over the claims of God in the Bible. They judged for themselves which parts of the Bible were true, and which parts were myths. In some cases, following the beliefs of Newton and his closed system creation, all miracles were thrown out as impossible, since not even God could violate the laws of nature he had set in place. Needless to say the new Bible volume of some of its critics became very slim indeed.

Another casualty of that period became the very triune God himself. Reasoning with Greek logic one could not be three, and three could not be one. How God could be a lone person and yet be the God who is love, unless he was a narcissist, they did not consider. Thus the triune God was reduced to one person who had only himself to love and who was out there watching us, and letting us get on with things.

Robert observed that for many years the theological and devotional books written after the Reformation, even by those who believed in the Trinity, seemed to have little understanding of the practical implication of this reality. The doctrine of the Trinity was often relegated to a minor part, in the great scheme of things, but that was changing. Melvyn and Robert were excited about the resurgence of Trinitarian theology among many followers of Christ. They revelled in their discussions and in the beauty of their relationship in the triune God, who let them share in the circle of his love, and directed their lives and thinking through his Spirit.

Chapter Nineteen

Melvyn visits Karen

Six months after his return home from hospital Melvyn actually made the long trip to see Karen and her family, and stayed a few days. Wisely he came on a Monday since the four children were in school during the day, and he could cope with their high spirits and enjoy their company without getting too fatigued, when they got home each day.

On the Tuesday when Adam had left for work, Karen was surprised to find her father asking her if she would join him in the sitting room, as he had something serious to discuss with her. She became somewhat apprehensive as she had been hurt by his words on so many previous occasions. She knew that if she tried to disclose her hurt, as she had on many occasions, she was likely to get the brush off with excuses such as: "I was only trying to help you. I was giving you constructive criticism."

She sat beside him and waited. Melvyn initiated the conversation:

"You know, Karen, that I had some very vivid dreams about life after death when I was in hospital. It was not at all what I expected. My impression from what I had been taught as a child was that the bodiless spirits of believers would be transported to heaven, after their death here. I believed they would there take part in a very few so-called holy activities such as worshipping God, and maybe meeting loved ones who had gone on before. After the resurrection and judgement, unbelievers would be consigned to hell and its horrors, while believers would get to live in heaven in their new bodies. The activities they engaged in would be mostly the same as those they performed before the resurrection.

There was talk of a huge celebration called the wedding feast of the lamb, but apart from that, it just seemed that this endless round of worship services would continue. Of course there were to be plusses in that disease, sadness, and deprivations of every kind were to be abolished, but it all seemed very tame and uninteresting to me.

Instead, in my dreams, I was shown a most amazing king, wonderfully approachable and yet utterly majestic and exalted, a king who came off his throne to wipe away tears. It was beyond words. His kingdom of love flowed out of him, with freedom, hope, health, friendship, conviviality, living and learning, fun, and all the good things we enjoy on earth, without any of the downside. It was good beyond what any mind on earth could imagine, and I only had a little taste of it. Immanuel, that's what he liked to be called, made it quite clear that I lacked the capacity at this stage, to comprehend much of what was going on. Indeed he hinted that the revelation would continue to amaze and further thrill his people, as they developed their capacity to enjoy life in the triune circle for eternity.

Karen, I feel I have to write this book about life after death, about what I was shown in my dreams and visions, but I am still very confused. You see there seem to be so many ideas out there about what is really going to happen, once we're dead, but before our actual resurrection."

"That's amazing, Dad. It's thrilling and I know it has changed your life. You must tell me more, but I know what you mean, Dad, about life after death. I thought I had it all worked out but the more I read the Bible, the more I begin to feel that I know nothing at all, about that stage of our being. All the books out there are so contradictory and seem to make no sense to me. I am actually beginning to wonder if they are just a ruse of the Evil One, to get us distracted by irrelevancies that keep us from focusing on the really important things. Jesus castigated the religious folks of his day, who were careful to tithe mint and cumin, and forgot the weightier matters like justice and mercy that were the closest concerns of God's heart," Karen replied.

"I was given no insight into what happens immediately after death before we are given our resurrection bodies. From my reading of the Bible it seems to me that a lot of what people think still has to happen at the end times, has already taken place. A lot of the dire warnings Jesus gave in the Gospels were fulfilled in the fall of Jerusalem in AD70. That was one of the bloodiest times in history, not only in Jerusalem but also in Rome. Christ said these terrible things would happen before the generation he was addressing had passed on; so it can't refer to the end of time.

Also, much of what is recorded in the book of Revelation has already been fulfilled. People don't seem to realize the type of literature John was producing. These events were not sequential things, but a panorama of visions and prophecies to give encouragement to the persecuted Christians at the time. They understood the significance of the images better than we do. Of course, the pictures of the complete victory of Christ over the dominion of darkness, is encouragement to persecuted Christians in every age."

"Then, Dad, I don't think you need to worry about the in between times up to the last judgement. Your book can only be about life after our bodies are resurrected, and we're living on the new earth."

"You're right, Karen. That is the reality that is waiting for us, and I had a tiny foretaste of it. There is going to be a new earth and a new heaven. Actually heaven, God's dwelling place, the New Jerusalem, is going to descend to earth. The two are to be joined under the rule of King Jesus who will hand the kingdom over to his Father. Somehow we will rule with him over the earth and take care of it, as we were meant to do before humanity sinned."

Over the next couple of hours Melvyn shared with Karen some of the extraordinary sights and sounds, life and love, fun and laughter, service and joy that he had experienced in his amazing dreams.

"What I saw was only what my limited, seeing through a glass darkly, imagination could accommodate. As Immanuel told me there is much, much more, but my mind could not grasp it yet. The visions were only fleeting shadows of the reality," Melvyn explained.

"Yet it was amazing, Dad, and you do need to get it written down to encourage people to start living in the kingdom now. It brings such joy and liberation to be walking hand in hand with the Spirit of Christ, and as we get to know Christ better, we become able to participate deeper and deeper, in the joyful life of the triune God of love."

"Yes, indeed! Christ commended the faithful servants in the parable of the talents and invited them to share in the joy of his life."

"Yes, Dad, go for it! It is something you must do!"